BORDER LEGEND TRILOGY

THE TALL MAN

BOOK 1

LEE BISHOP

WCP

World Castle Publishing, LLC
Pensacola, Florida

Copyright © Lee Bishop 2014
Print ISBN: 9781629891507
eBook ISBN: 9781629891514
First Edition World Castle Publishing, LLC, October 1, 2014
http://www.worldcastlepublishing.com

Licensing Notes

Cover: Karen Fuller
Photos: Shutterstock
Editor: Maxine Bringenberg

DEDICATION

This novel is dedicated to my wife, Sue, who is truly a
wonderful woman.

CHAPTER 1

The group of ten vaqueros rode their horses slowly up the dry wash, moving in snake-like fashion around boulders, mesquite, and chaparral. Their leader, Ricardo Montoya, held up his hand, and the horsemen stopped and dismounted. He motioned for them to move against the side of the arroyo. Most of the men sprawled on the sand and pulled their ponchos close about them.

They had been alternately walking and riding all night to reach the rear of the Apache band. The Indians had stolen nearly thirty horses from the hacienda of Don Diego Salazar the day before. Now they waited for the shooting to begin when the main party of Mexican cowboys attacked the Apache camp. Ricardo and his men would then shoot the Indians guarding the horses and cut off the Apaches' escape.

Ricardo looked at the sky and saw the first streaks of light in the east. The attack would begin in about a half hour, as soon as there was enough light for the Mexicans to clearly see their targets. The Apaches, estimated to be about twenty in number, had jumped the San Carlos Indian Reservation in the Arizona Territory.

Strangely, the scouts had reported that the Apaches were traveling with their families. Most raiders worked together in

1

a fast moving band that could strike, kill, and quickly move on. This group apparently wanted to establish a new life with their families included. The Salazar horses would make them mobile and independent. Just by chance, one of the Salazar vaqueros had seen the Apaches rounding up the horses on the Don's northern range and had ridden to the rancho with the news.

Ricardo slipped off his poncho and sombrero and dropped them on the ground. Most of the vaqueros followed his example. Then, he walked down the line whispering last minute instructions to his men. The cowboys checked their weapons. Montoya climbed up and over the lip of the gully, making his way through the scrub brush and boulders to a small rise. Ahead and slightly below him were the horses.

Two Apaches sat on their haunches talking quietly with one another. Ricardo motioned to his men and pointed to the positions he wanted them to take. The vaqueros quietly obeyed. He could just see the edge of the camp fifty yards on the other side of the horses. Montoya had picked the best riflemen from among Don Diego's vaqueros to participate in the hunt, and he felt confident.

A fusillade of gunfire exploded in the quiet of the early morning. The two Apaches jumped to their feet, and Ricardo shot one through the back. The Indian pitched forward and landed like a cat on his hands and knees, then fell forward on his face. The second Indian turned and fired just as a volley of shots rang out from Montoya's men. He was propelled backwards by the force of the bullets and fell on his back, dead.

The firing became heavy from the camp, mingled with screams from the Indians and yells from the vaqueros. Suddenly, a group of Apaches burst into full view as they ran for the horses. Montoya and his men fired another volley, and four of the Indians went down. The other braves jumped down behind rock outcroppings and mesquite bushes and returned fire.

All of Montoya's men were shooting now, and the Indians returned the gunfire. One of the vaqueros was thrown backwards by the force of a bullet that struck him in the shoulder.

Several of the Apaches ran off, jumped down into another arroyo, and disappeared. "Alfredo! Manuel!" Ricardo yelled to the men closest to him. "Follow me!"

Montoya ducked down and ran towards the twisting gulley to a point where he believed he could intercept the escaping Apaches. He reached the edge and saw them below just as the Indians spotted him. One of the Apaches went down as Montoya fired his revolver. A rifle slug grazed Ricardo's arm as he lost his footing and tumbled into the arroyo.

In a split second, a warrior was on him, and the Apache's knife arm flashed downward. Ricardo grabbed his arm and they rolled over in the sand. Montoya was on the bottom, but he used his feet and managed to throw the Indian over his head. Ricardo grabbed his own knife from its scabbard. The two men crouched down, facing one another, oblivious to the fighting going on around them.

The brave's face was painted with black streaks under the eyes and across the cheeks. His dark eyes glittered with hatred. The Apache dived forward and thrust his knife in an effort to disembowel Montoya. Ricardo jumped to one side, and the Indian's knife slashed the outside of his leg.

The Apache was back on his feet immediately and rushed Montoya again, slashing at his throat. Ricardo jumped back as the knife blade just missed his neck. As if by reflex, the Mexican leader buried his knife in the Indian's exposed side.

The Apache gave a deep grunt and dropped to his knees, his face twisted in pain. He stared at Montoya, moaned, and rolled over on the ground, attempting to get to his feet once more as Ricardo shot him through the head.

The battle still raged around him. One of the Apaches fired his rifle, and the bullet struck Alfredo Cabrillo in the face. The vaquero's lifeless body fell into the arroyo. The Mexicans and Apaches were now firing at each other at close range. Two more Apaches went down. A third warrior nimbly climbed up the side of the gully and disappeared.

Firing slackened now as the vaqueros closed in on the last three braves cornered in the wide drainage channel. One Apache was halfway up the side of a rocky incline firing from behind a boulder. Another of Montoya's men was shot dead. Ricardo sent his vaqueros to the right and left in an effort to outflank the warrior. They traded gunfire with the Apache, and he rolled down the incline.

He used the same maneuvering technique to kill a second brave. A third Apache managed to retreat out of the arroyo and fled.

The shooting finally stopped, and Montoya stood up and silently looked at the bodies strewn around him like dolls. The tall man slowly walked over to another of the fallen vaqueros and gently turned him over. He was dead.

Ricardo shook his head. *Where did they get all of their rifles?* He wondered.

A body count revealed four dead Mexicans and two wounded, while sixteen Apaches had died. Montoya supposed that three or four warriors had escaped. Ten Apache women and children were rounded up and herded together. The squaws began their death chants, and the wailing made Ricardo's stomach churn.

Four good men dead, Montoya thought, including his friend, Alfredo. He knelt beside the body of his boyhood friend and said a quick prayer.

Minutes later, Don Diego Salazar and his group of private bodyguards rode up. Montoya's vaqueros began yelling and firing their guns in the air to salute their patron. He magnanimously raised his hand in receipt of their tribute.

Salazar was, as usual, dressed in black and was mounted on a beautiful black stallion. He wore a ruffled white silk shirt, black satin jacket with gold embroidery, and black leather pants and chaps. Solid gold buttons ran up his leggings and adorned his jacket in two rows. The stallion's saddle and accessories were equally ornate. The horse and rider cast a magnificent image. No *hacendado* in the State of Sonora compared with Salazar when it came to fine clothing.

The Don looked around with an air of arrogant self-confidence. In his mid-fifties, Salazar was still trim and handsome, although his face was heavily lined, and he appeared to be in pain much of the time. He had dark eyes, a black mustache, and a black Vandyke beard. His hair was graying slightly at the temples, giving him a distinguished look.

Don Diego was not a large man, but his lack of physical stature was more than offset by an iron will that turned to ferocity when annoyed, and calculating cruelty when challenged. All who lived on the vast hacienda feared Salazar's wrath. His legendary cruelty was largely responsible for the well-kept order on his huge land holdings, which approached nearly two hundred thousand acres.

Ricardo was a level-headed, sharp thinking man who had grown up on the ranch and quickly advanced to the position of *Segundo,* or foreman, and general manager.

But recently, Salazar had been changing Montoya's orders to the men as if by whim. He would chastise Ricardo in front of the men for no good reason, and severely criticize Montoya for being responsible for mistakes that Salazar himself had made. Ricardo took the rebukes in silence, suspecting that the patron was jealous of Montoya's power among the men.

Montoya was considering asking the Don for a change of assignment away from the main ranch when the Apaches jumped the reservation. Don Diego had accepted Ricardo's plan of attack and then announced it to the vaqueros as his own. Salazar never entered into fighting. He viewed himself as more of a general than a private. Besides, there was the danger of being shot.

Ricardo walked confidently towards Salazar, stopping next to the black stallion to exchange greetings.

"Sixteen Apaches are dead, Don Diego. Four of your vaqueros have died gallantly."

"It was a victory I deserved," Salazar declared. Don Diego looked over at the small group of women and children huddled together, wailing for their dead husbands and fathers. "You were told that no prisoners were to be taken!" Salazar said loudly.

Montoya glanced at the Apaches, then returned his gaze to Salazar. "We took no warriors captive. The wounded were put to death," Ricardo stated.

"My orders were no captives!" Salazar shouted.

"These are women and children," Montoya said quietly, yet firmly.

"They are animals. They multiply like lice."

Montoya gave Salazar a skeptical look, but said nothing.

Don Diego's eyes blazed as he looked down at Montoya. A smile spread across his face. "You have your orders, Montoya. Carry them out!"

Ricardo's face hardened and his eyes narrowed. "Surely it will not be difficult to send these wretches back to the reservation."

"Do you challenge my authority?" he growled.

"Of course not, Don Diego. I'm asking you to reconsider," Ricardo stated.

Salazar was visibly angry. "Carry out your orders," he shouted.

Ricardo exhaled deeply. He hooked his thumbs in his gun belt and looked at the ground. *So, it is to end this way*, he thought. The patron wanted this confrontation, and the Apaches were the tool he would use.

About thirty vaqueros had gathered in a large circle around the men. Ricardo raised his eyes and looked at the men. He saw confusion and fear etched on their faces. Montoya made his decision. He fixed his eyes on Salazar.

"I'll not kill women and children for you or any man," Ricardo stated in a loud, clear voice.

Don Diego looked shocked. No one ever disobeyed his orders, and for Ricardo to do so in front of the vaqueros was a terrible insult. The black-clad patron was furious. He lashed out with his quirt and struck Montoya across the neck and down the back. Then, he raised his whip and swung a second time.

Ricardo grabbed the braided leather lash and yanked on it. Salazar nearly flew out of his saddle, and his horse reared. The landowner fought to stay in the saddle and keep his horse under control. Once this was accomplished, he was going to grab his revolver, but one glance at Montoya's face and he changed his mind. Ricardo's eyes were mere slits and his jaw was set.

Salazar looked around at his men. "Now, hear this! This man, Ricardo Montoya, has disgraced me! I hereby strip him of all his rank and privileges!" Don Diego looked down at Montoya. "Go back to the ranch and stay there until I return. At that time, I will determine what punishment you shall receive!" he said in an angry voice.

Montoya turned and walked over to his horse.

"Pedro Gomez!" the patron yelled in a loud voice.

From the ranks of his private bodyguards, a huge man spurred his horse forward.

Gomez had a bearlike body with big arms and legs, and a huge stomach that crowded his saddle horn. Two great bushy eyebrows, a grotesque red nose, a stringy beard and mustache, and a mouthful of rotting teeth characterized the unforgettable face. He smelled as bad as he looked, and was known for his brutish, almost uncivilized behavior. Gomez possessed the simplistic mind of a child, always blindly obedient to his orders.

"Pedro," Salazar said in a voice loud enough for all to hear. "My orders were no prisoners!"

Gomez's pig-like eyes lit up. He pulled a long machete from a scabbard tied to his horse's saddle.

"Let me be the one, Don Diego!" he bellowed.

***

Ricardo stopped his horse at the crest of a large hill and looked out across the enormous rolling plains a mile above sea level. Small groups of mountains dotted the horizon. In the distant background, he could just make out the beginning of the Sierra Madre mountain range sweeping south into the heart of Mexico.

Below him he could see the tiny dots that were Don Diego's cattle grazing on the lush grass. The endless sea of gold was broken here and there by groves of oak and walnut trees, and clumps of thorny shrubs. Spiny chaparral and mesquite became more plentiful in the foothills of the mountains and on the smaller rocky hills.

Montoya loved the ranch country, its Spartan life, and the simple pleasures of the range. He dismounted, rolled a cigarette, and smoked as he looked out over the countryside. Ricardo contemplated what would happen to him now. He expected the patron to banish him to one of the outlying ranch properties, but he welcomed the exile.

Montoya's rise through the ranks to top operations officer and adviser to Salazar had been swift. Ten years earlier, Don Diego had just begun to build his empire, and his instincts had been good. He had gathered around him the bravest and most intelligent vaqueros. They had fought to clear the land of Apaches and *bandidos*, gradually shaping the hacienda into one of the largest in northern Mexico.

Ricardo had saved Salazar's life during a skirmish with the Indians. An Apache had knocked Don Diego off his horse and was about to knife him when Montoya shot the Indian. Soon afterwards, Ricardo had been appointed head of the detachment of private bodyguards. Montoya's ability to speak and write the English language had enabled him to accompany Salazar's entourage across the border into the Arizona Territory. Ricardo had learned the art of bargaining during cattle and gold transactions.

Don Diego himself refused to speak English. The patron believed it was beneath his dignity to associate with gringos. Ricardo's advice and shrewd business dealings had proved to be extremely profitable for Salazar. Soon, the wealthy

Mexican rancher had stopped traveling to the foreign country altogether.

As gold, silver, and copper mining began to boom in both the Arizona Territory and Sonora, the demand for beef had peaked at the mines. The Apaches had never been successfully contained, and more and more cavalry units were stationed at forts north of the international boundary. Beef sold to the forts also was at peak prices. Salazar's empire solidified, and the Apaches could not penetrate the stronghold that Ricardo Montoya planned and built for the patron.

But, as the challenges had become fewer, Don Diego's personality had changed. His arrogance and petty indulgences were more pronounced. His neighbors, who once admired his cunning and bold moves, began to dislike his unreasonableness, frequent demands, insolence, and total disregard for the well-being of others.

As Don Diego's personality and moral values began their steady decline, Ricardo's reputation for honesty and fairness had grown. The neighboring landowners now preferred to do business with Montoya, and even asked his advice in dealings north of the border.

Only during the past year had Salazar's tirades touched Ricardo. Always before, Don Diego had been intelligent enough not to embarrass or criticize the man who oversaw the smooth operation of his empire. But, now there was little that Ricardo could do. The *hacendado* ruled the lives of all people who lived on his lands, peon and vaquero alike. They lived in bondage on the patron's lands in an almost medieval form of serfdom. Everything on his land, including the people, belonged to Don Diego. This also included all crops, housing, and animals. Ricardo Montoya was not free to leave and could be forcibly brought back if he tried.

Ricardo was mulling over the alternatives in his mind when he heard distant gunshots. The barely audible gunfire was coming from the opposite direction of the clash with the Apaches. Montoya sensed that some people had encountered trouble on the road from Nogales. He ground out his cigarette, swung into the saddle, and rode down the hill at a gallop.

LEE BISHOP

CHAPTER 2

Ricardo and his palomino thundered down one hill and up another, weaving in and out between clumps of mesquite, chaparral, and cactus. Montoya guided his stallion with just the slightest touch of his knees, and the horse responded instantly. The two were as one pounding up and down the rocky terrain.

When they reached the flats covered by a sea of grass, he gave the horse its head and Oro surged forward, enjoying the freedom of galloping unchecked. The shots became louder as they approached the road stretching southward from Nogales into Mexico. Here the land began a gentle downward trend leading into a valley ringed with rocky hills.

Commanding a view of the countryside as he rode out of the high country, Ricardo could make out a coach and saw that one of its team was down. Another horse was lying dead in the road a few feet away. Puffs of smoke came from *banditos'* guns as they fired down on their victims, who were trapped under a huge rock outcropping beside the roadway.

At least two defenders were still firing at the outlaws. Ricardo swung down from the saddle even before his horse came to a complete halt. He climbed to a vantage point between two boulders and saw at a glance that the battle would last only a few more minutes. The ornate carriage, he surmised, belonged to an important person or family, and they were caught in an ambush.

Montoya aimed at the back of one of the bandits directly in front and slightly below him. He fired his Winchester, and the Mexican yelled and pitched forward. Ricardo levered another shell into the rifle's chamber and snapped off a shot as the second outlaw crouched down next to his dead companion. The bullet struck the second outlaw in the side, and the impact of the slug knocked him to the ground. The wounded bandit had two belts of cartridges crisscrossing his chest. He yelled a warning to his companions and fired a return shot at Montoya. The bullet went wild.

Three other outlaws were on Ricardo's side of the road. They all quickly shifted their attention to him. He moved behind one of the large rocks as a hail of bullets came in his direction. Ricardo ducked down and ran to his left to get to a better vantage point. He half-slid, half-ran down an incline to get behind a large boulder, just as one of the outlaws came around the other side. Montoya's momentum propelled him straight into the surprised bandit.

The outlaw's eyes widened, and a look of surprise came over his features. Ricardo smashed his rifle butt into the bearded face. The bandit's head snapped back and his sombrero flew off as he pitched over backwards.

Montoya knew there were only two bandits left on his side of the road. He set down his rifle and drew his revolver for close combat. From above him, a big man dressed in dark pants and a jacket fired down on Ricardo. The slug sliced along his back, but it was not a serious wound. Ricardo jumped forward and rolled out of sight.

One of the travelers pinned down under the rock outcropping fired at the big outlaw, who had exposed himself in order to get a better shot at Montoya. The slug hit the bandit in the lower back and knocked him off the boulder. He screamed just before he smashed into the ground.

The final outlaw yelled a warning to his companions across the road and ran for his horse. The outlaws on the other side of the road decided that they no longer wished to continue and disappeared from sight. They mounted and rode away.

Montoya's leg throbbed from the wound the Apache had inflicted earlier, and now his back felt like it was on fire. Minutes passed, and there was no more gunfire. Ricardo scouted around the boulders on his side of the road, and then called over to the people in hiding.

"It's all right! I'm a friend! Check the rocks on the other side of the road," Montoya called out.

Ricardo stood atop one of the boulders while a vaquero from the ambushed party scouted among the rocks. After a few minutes, the cowboy waved his rifle to signify that all was safe. Montoya made his way down to the trapped group. At close range, he recognized the coach.

Don Carlos Bustamante, the landowner living directly to the west of Don Diego's land, helped his daughter, Maria, from their hiding place.

"I thought I recognized your carriage, Don Carlos," said Ricardo.

Bustamante's eyes flashed and a huge smile spread across his broad face. He had silver hair and a silver beard. Don Carlos was known for his friendly disposition and frequent laughter.

"Ricardo!" the patron bellowed. "I might have known it was you."

Maria Bustamante straightened up and dusted off her calfskin riding outfit. She loosened the chin strap and took off her broad-brimmed felt hat. She was in a daze and looked around with expressionless eyes. Her gaze settled on Ricardo as he approached her.

"Hello, Ricardo," she said in a confused voice. It took her several minutes to return to the present and push the nightmare from her mind.

"It's nice to see you, Maria," said Ricardo. He immediately recognized the ridiculousness of his statement.

Bustamante grabbed Montoya's hand and shook it strongly.

"Am I glad to see you. I thought they had us for a while. Those buzzards learned their lessons this time," said Bustamante in rapid-fire fashion.

The ranch owner suddenly realized his daughter was in shock and helped her climb into the coach out of the sun. The Bustamantes' remaining vaquero hitched his horse to the coach in place of the dead animal. The driver and two of the Don's vaqueros had died in the first blaze of gunfire. Their bodies were placed to one side of the road and covered with a tarp. Three of the four outlaws that Montoya had shot were dead, and Ricardo dispatched the fourth man.

"We were just on our way back to the rancho. I sold some cattle to the United States Army," said Bustamante. "They must have known that I had gold."

Ricardo took off his sombrero and ran his fingers through his thick, black hair.

"Can you trust the remaining vaquero?" he asked in a low voice.

The silver-haired Bustamante looked intently at Ricardo.

"I would trust him with my life. He's been with me forever," said the patron.

"He's the only one of your group left alive," Montoya pointed out.

"I know. But he's not the one," the rancher stated.

Montoya could see that the patron was unswerving in his loyalty to his rider.

"I'll accompany you back to your ranch," Ricardo said.

"That would be appreciated," said Don Carlos. "But, your employer won't like it. Don Diego has never liked me."

"Whether or not he likes it makes no difference anymore," Montoya stated.

The rancher perceived a note of bitterness in Montoya's voice. After a moment, Ricardo explained what had occurred and how he was being sent back to the rancho in disgrace. Bustamante's eyes were riveted on Montoya as he told the story.

Don Carlos shook his head in disbelief. "He had the women and children put to death?"

"Yes," said Ricardo. "I don't know the man anymore. It's as if he's crazy with power."

Montoya scouted ahead of the carriage and then backtracked to determine if they were being followed. As the coach bounced over the rutted trail, Ricardo felt sorry for Maria. Continually being bumped and thrashed around wouldn't do her much good on top of the fright she had just experienced, Montoya reasoned. She was not a woman accustomed to violence.

***

Actually, the jolting ride had brought the raven-haired beauty out of her stupor. Her senses were no longer dulled, and she assured her father that she had recovered.

Maria Bustamante possessed a fragile beauty. She had an oval face, high cheek bones, straight nose, and full lips. Adding to her beauty were her long black hair and magnificent grey eyes. She had a full figure and a graceful movement about her.

Much to her father's dismay, none of the young men suited her. Don Carlos had turned down nearly half a dozen proposals of marriage on behalf of his daughter. It had become an embarrassing problem for him.

She pulled back the flap from the carriage window when she heard Ricardo's horse come alongside. Maria studied the tall vaquero, who sat straight in the saddle and moved as if he was part of the horse.

Ricardo yelled something to the driver and continued to ride beside the coach. They had met frequently at fiestas, weddings, social gatherings, and holidays, but Ricardo was always stiff and formal, exchanging only polite greetings with her. Montoya was not a member of the privileged ruling class and never overstepped the bounds of propriety. She gazed at his profile with his broad chin, strong nose, and curly black hair, admiring his size. At well over six feet tall, Ricardo was half a head taller than most men. He had a large torso and firm, lean build.

Ricardo turned his head and looked into her eyes. He held her gaze for a moment, and a disconcerting feeling passed over her. For the first time she realized he was looking at her as being a desirable woman, and he made no effort to hide his feelings. She did not look away. Maria felt aroused and had a strong desire to reach out and touch him. Her emotions suddenly were in turmoil, because the excitement of the moment was thrilling. *What's wrong with me?* She thought. *Has this attack disrupted my senses, or is it him?*

His intense look continued for a few moments more, and then he touched his knees to the palomino and the horse bounded ahead.

***

It was almost dusk before they covered the nearly twenty miles between the ambush site and the Bustamante rancho.

Several armed vaqueros rode out to meet the coach a mile from the hacienda, escorting it through the gate and into the courtyard. Most of the rooms emptied out into the central, open courtyard and smaller covered patio at the far end.

The exterior walls of the fortress were eighteen feet high, nearly two feet thick, and were made of adobe. A parapet walkway ran around the top of the building on all four sides of the interior. This gave the vaqueros excellent vantage positions for firing at Apaches during major attacks. The only openings in the house were narrow gun ports that pierced the outer walls. The ranch lay directly in the path of the White Mountain and Chiricahua Apache routes for raiding into Mexico.

Wooden floors ran around the base of the walls, and the eaves overhead protected the floors from rain and the windows from direct sunlight. The courtyard contained a well and a windmill, and had a water-storage tower alongside. If a sustained siege would take place, the house and courtyard would be able to supply all of the necessities of life to Bustamante and his vaqueros.

The Bustamante ranch house was built in the center of a complex of structures. A large adobe corral, which could hold several hundred head of cattle, was located to the north. Smaller corrals nearby held horses for the family members and cowboys.

A large wooden barn stood to the east of the hacienda; there was a mill for grinding grain, a blacksmith's shop, slaughterhouse, and a bunkhouse for fifty vaqueros. Dotting the landscape around the main ranch complex were single level and two story adobe buildings used by peon families. They were simple adobe brick buildings with dirt floors and flat mud roofs.

Ricardo dismounted with some pain and stiffness, but his face showed no sign of discomfort. He stood and watched as Maria was helped from the coach. Her eyes sought him out, and he felt a stirring deep within himself. He knew he was becoming enamored. She was quickly whisked away by a flock of noisy attendants.

"Ricardo, once you have rested, perhaps you can join me for a drink? Say, in about two hours?" said Bustamante.

"It would be my pleasure, Don Carlos."

Montoya was led to a large bedroom at the south end of the ranch house, where a tub filled with hot water awaited him. The wounds on his arm and back were minor, but they stung in the hot water. He groaned as he let himself stretch out in the long, metal tub. A peon knocked and entered with a tray of various kinds of foods.

"How may I serve you?" the small Mexican asked.

"Brandy and a cigar would be nice," Ricardo said, and smiled.

He ate and then smoked a cigar while the water took out the soreness. After the bath, the peon wrapped his wounds in clean bandages and laid out a fresh set of clothing. Surprisingly, the dark blue pants and matching jacket did not fit badly.

Ricardo crossed the courtyard and was led down a short hallway to Don Carlos's office. The elder man rose from behind his desk and motioned for Montoya to sit in one of the two large chairs in front of the fireplace.

"Thank you for your hospitality," said Ricardo.

The silver-haired patron looked at Montoya and then at the blazing fire. "There is no way I can properly thank you for saving my life and that of my daughter. We are deeply in your debt."

Montoya looked at the Don. "I'm glad I was near and able to help."

Bustamante was quiet for a moment, and both men sipped their drinks.

"I hope you will allow me to be frank," said Don Carlos.

"Of course," Ricardo replied.

"I do not think it is wise for you to return to the Salazar ranch," the Don said quietly.

"It's my home," Montoya stated.

Bustamante turned his head and inspected the tall vaquero.

"You and I both know that Don Diego can be vicious. You refused to carry out his orders. And worse, you confronted him and almost threw him to the ground in front of his men. He must be furious. Never have I met a more cruel individual. I fear he will do great harm to you, and possibly even kill you should you return."

Ricardo thought for a moment. "It may not be that bad. I worked hard for him for many years, and even saved his life during one battle. He trusted me with his most important business dealings in the Arizona Territory. This history should mean something to him."

"It should," said Don Carlos. "But, I fear that it won't. The man is too vain, too arrogant to remember what others have done for him."

Ricardo took a drink and then set the glass down. "My brother and father are there. I have no choice but to return. My brother, Rafael, is head of the hacienda guards."

The older man grunted. "He's collected quite an army and built himself a fortress. Next, he'll declare himself a king."

"There are several hundred people spread throughout the ranch, line camps, and outlying farming areas. Don Diego is running over twenty thousand cattle plus bringing thousands more range cattle to the ranch to be sent north to the Arizona Territory. It's a never ending shuttle of cattle northward."

Bustamante slowly shook his head. "No wonder he wants my pastureland on the west side of the Concepcion River."

"He was very angry when you refused his offer to buy the land," said Montoya.

"I wouldn't sell it to him at any price. I need that grazing land for my own cattle. And, even if I didn't, I would never let him enlarge his holdings at my expense," the Don said in a hard voice.

"Be careful," Ricardo warned. "He threatens to take the land at any cost."

"The government would frown on a confrontation between us. I imagine that the Army would be sent in to stop it," said the ranch owner. "But, to get back to our earlier conversation, I have a good friend with a large ranch outside of Ciudad Juarez. He would find that your experience in the United States would be very helpful to him. I believe you could have a top position in his business dealings. Would you like me to talk with him?"

"Your offer is very gracious. But, I must go back," Ricardo stated.

Later that evening, Maria Bustamante and Ricardo Montoya walked slowly around the hacienda grounds, followed closely by a large, formidable maiden aunt. Aunt Anna never took her eyes off the pair and never smiled.

They walked through the flower gardens and Ricardo was impressed by some of the largest roses he had ever seen. The gardens were ablaze with lanterns.

"It is a pleasure to have a guest here," said Maria.

Ricardo had a difficult time taking his eyes off the young woman long enough to examine the flowers. Maria wore a long, flowered dress and white shawl. A white jeweled comb accented her raven hair and creamy complexion. A strong sexual desire filled him as her melodic voice and perfume cast an almost hypnotic spell over Ricardo.

"Your hospitality is greatly appreciated," he replied.

Her eyes were frank, probing Montoya for answers to her unspoken questions. "How much longer can you stay?"

"I'll leave tomorrow," said Ricardo.

She clipped a brilliant red rose and handed it to him, but said nothing as she gazed into his eyes.

"I'll think of you when I see red roses," said Montoya.

Her eyes met his, and neither one looked away. Ricardo felt a churning in his stomach and his throat was dry. He was frustrated and deeply disappointed that he could not take her in his arms and kiss her passionately, but he could almost feel her Aunt Anna breathing down his neck. "I don't know when I will be back, but I will return," he said quietly.

"My prayers will be with you," Maria replied.

The ponderous maiden aunt broke up the intimacy of the moment with the announcement that it looked like rain and they should start back. Montoya examined the sky, but there were no clouds and the stars shined brightly.

LEE BISHOP

CHAPTER 3

El Rancho Grande was a magnificent white fortress atop a hill overlooking surrounding valleys and the Sonora River. The two-story ranch house was built around its own courtyard in the center of a maze of smaller buildings. Two trails wound up the hill from opposite sides. At the base of the hill were corrals, vegetable gardens, groves of fruit trees, and a proliferation of small adobe houses for the peons, set out in a ring more than a mile in diameter. Smaller fertile hills fell away from the center of El Rancho Grande, giving approaching travelers the impression of a white castle amid a sea of green and gold plots of land.

Don Diego's office and bedroom were on the top floor of the ranch house. An outer balcony circled the two rooms and allowed Salazar to leisurely survey his vast domain from any angle. He enjoyed the feeling of openness and freedom, along with the sense that he was defended from all sides against Apaches. More than one hundred families lived on the rancho, providing the Don with his own private work force and army.

Over the past five years, Ricardo Montoya had been the organizer and general manager for the complex. There were always four or five work parties busy erecting buildings, tearing down and moving others, clearing land, building smooth trails for coaches, and constructing corrals.

Ricardo rode his palomino along the main trail as it wound up the hill to the ranch house, exchanging greetings with several vaqueros who were leaving the center of the complex.

"Have you been to your father's house?" one of the ranch hands asked.

"No," Ricardo stated.

"Then you do not know. Your father is gravely ill. Vaqueros have been trying to locate you."

Montoya turned his horse and rode at a gallop around the outside wall of the ranch house until he reached the far side of the complex. He dismounted and quickly walked into the white adobe building where he and his brother, Rafael, lived with his father, Gustavo. His father was a master woodcrafter.

Ricardo opened the ornately carved door and walked into the main room. The house had wooden floors instead of mud and was filled with an abundance of wood furniture made by his father.

A fat, grey-haired woman rose from one of the chairs. "Thank God, you have come in time!"

"What has happened, Leona?"

The older woman's eyes were red from crying and lack of sleep.

"We thought he had a bad chest cold. Then, shortly after you left, he took to his bed and has gotten worse. The doctor came and…." The housekeeper began crying again.

Ricardo put his arm around her shoulders. "What did the doctor say?" Ricardo asked in a concerned voice.

She looked at him with tear-filled eyes. "He said your father is dying!"

Ricardo was shocked and flinched inadvertently. Leona began weeping again as he tried to compose himself.

"He hasn't much time left," she said.

Ricardo nodded and walked over and opened his father's bedroom door. He was shocked a second time as he looked at his father. In just a few days' time, the old man appeared to have withered. His skin was white and wrinkled, his breathing was labored, and his eyes were sunken and red.

Ricardo reached down, grabbed the old man's shoulders, and embraced him. He gritted his teeth, trying to hold back the tears.

"I'm glad you are here," his father gasped. "I had to see you one last time. There's something you must know."

Gustavo stopped to catch his breath. He was emaciated, and his short, gray beard looked too large for his shrunken face.

"Don't try to talk, Father," Ricardo said in a soft voice.

"I'll be gone in a few hours, so just listen," he rasped. "It was twenty-six years ago. I was on a trip for the patron in the Arizona Territory. I was camped off the road and was just packing my gear when I heard gunfire. I ran through the trees to the top of a small hill and saw a stagecoach being fired at. I didn't have a gun. A woman ran in my direction with a small child in her arms. She hid the child in the rocks and then ran away."

The old man halted to catch his breath. Perspiration stood out on his forehead, and a rasping sound came from his throat.

"Save your strength, Father," Ricardo implored the old man.

Gustavo shook his head. "I must finish," he said in a strained voice.

A helpless feeling came over Ricardo.

The elder Montoya continued. "This happened on the road between Nogales and Patagonia. I had left my rifle in the camp. The woman was only a few yards from me when a big man came into sight. He shot her with a rifle. She was killed instantly."

Gustavo was looking into his son's eyes as he spoke. Tears were running down Ricardo's face.

"The man had a long scar leading down his cheek and across his chin in an L-shape. When he checked the woman to see that she was dead, he was not more than ten yards from me. I couldn't move or make a sound, or I would have been next. Then, another man came in sight. He said, 'Don't forget to take the money so it looks like a robbery.'"

Ricardo pulled a chair up to the side of the bed, sat down, and held his father's hand.

"The second man wore two pearl-handled revolvers, and his holsters were black. They started searching around. I knew they were looking for the boy, but they never found him. Later, after I heard them ride away, I went and looked."

Gustavo Montoya coughed and closed his eyes for a moment.

He continued in a weak voice. "The woman's husband had been killed. Mother of God, I couldn't believe white men could do such a thing."

Ricardo was in a state of confusion. His father was dying before his eyes. At the same time, he was telling him some strange story.

"I'm almost through," the old man whispered. "They burned part of the coach, but I could still make out the letters, C and B, in a crest. It was an important family. You could tell from the expensive clothing they wore."

Ricardo wiped his father's face with a wet cloth. "You couldn't have saved them. I realize that."

Gustavo's breathing was labored. He turned his head and looked out the window. "I located the boy. He had crawled back under a ledge. He didn't cry because he was in shock. I brought him back here to the hacienda, and your mother and I decided to raise him as our own."

Ricardo had a quizzical look on his face. "Father, I don't remember any boy…."

The old man was crying now as he gazed at his son. "That boy was you, Ricardo," he said in a raspy voice.

Ricardo's eyes narrowed, and an expression of pain crossed his face. He jumped up, knocking the chair over.

"No!" he said in a loud voice. "I don't want to hear anything like that."

"It's the truth. I swear it before God," his father said in a barely audible voice.

Ricardo smashed his fist down on the table next to the bed, sending everything onto the floor. "Why tell me such a crazy story?"

"I cannot die with it on my conscience. It doesn't matter, Ricardo. You are my son and you always will be. It made my heart sing to see you rise to such a high position. I love you more than life itself," Gustavo emphasized.

Ricardo stood before the bed staring at his father. His fists were clenched and his guts were churning.

"Does Rafael know?"

"No. Just your mother and I knew the truth, and she took the secret to her grave."

Gustavo suddenly shuddered painfully. Ricardo bent over his father.

"Did the doctor give you anything for the pain?" Ricardo asked.

"Yes, but it doesn't work well," he said in a soft voice once the pain subsided.

The door opened and Rafael walked into the room. He was two inches shorter than Ricardo and twenty pounds lighter. But, the two men looked much alike.

Rafael had gained a reputation in his own right for being a tough fighter who was brave in battles with the Apaches. He was very popular with his men, quick to joke and laugh, and intelligent. And, he loved the ladies. Rafael also had been chosen by Don Diego for advanced schooling in the English language and mathematics. He had risen to become the head of Salazar's private bodyguards at the same time that Ricardo had become Segundo at the hacienda.

He touched Ricardo on the shoulder and then knelt next to the bed and prayed. Rafael stood up and then bent over and kissed his father's cheek. It brought a weak smile to the old man's face.

"Father, can I get you anything?" Rafael asked.

The old man shook his head, no.

"I am very proud of you two boys. There are very few men who have the opportunity to see their sons achieve such success in life."

The two brothers glanced at each other with skepticism owing to the present circumstances.

"I have only one regret."

"What is it, Father?" Ricardo asked.

The elder Montoya smiled weakly. "Neither of you are very good woodworkers."

The brothers smiled. Their father always was humorous, even in difficult times.

"It doesn't matter that I'm going. I've had a full, happy life, and I'm ready to see your blessed mother again. I've missed her so much," said Gustavo.

Tears were running down both brothers' faces. They stayed with him until he fell asleep and then walked into the living room. Ricardo sat down in an overstuffed chair while Rafael sat on the couch.

"Is it true?" Rafael asked Ricardo.

"Yes. I couldn't order the killing of Apache women and children. And, no man beats me with a whip," he stated in a gruff voice.

Rafael gazed at his brother with concern. "Pedro Gomez was covered with blood when he got back here. The vaqueros said the man is sick. No one will go near him."

Ricardo said nothing and just stared out the window.

"Don Diego is not here. He left immediately for Hermosillo to celebrate his great victory," Rafael noted.

Ricardo still said nothing. Rafael was silent for a moment and studied his brother.

"What is it?" Rafael asked.

Ricardo looked intently at his brother. Then, he related the story to Rafael that he had just heard from his father.

Rafael was stunned, and his eyes were wide in disbelief. "That's impossible! It's crazy!"

Ricardo took a deep breath. "He didn't lie, and he was not hallucinating. His mind was clear even to small details."

"But, we look like brothers! We are brothers!" Rafael stated loudly.

"Of course we are, and we always will be brothers," Ricardo said. "Listen, something else happened that kept me from returning immediately."

Ricardo told his brother about the ambush of the Bustamante party.

"Did you spend some time with Maria?" Rafael asked.

Ricardo looked at his brother with suspicious eyes.

Rafael was smiling. "You can't hide it from me. I've seen the way you have secretly looked at her when you thought no one was watching. The strange thing, Brother, is that I saw her looking at you the same way."

Ricardo stood up and looked embarrassed. "You make too much of this."

Rafael laughed. "I know you. I've seen you with a lot of women. None of them ever affected you like she does."

"I'm hungry. Let's eat," said Ricardo in an abrupt manner.

They walked to one of the outside cooking fires. The peon woman attending the fire happily served the two men beef, beans, and tortillas. These men held positions of power, and she considered it a privilege that they chose to eat her food. Rafael slipped her a few pesos.

The brothers ate in silence and looked out over the green and gold rolling hills.

"This is the most beautiful spot in Mexico," said Ricardo.

Rafael glanced at his brother. "In time this will pass. The patron will eventually miss your advice and planning ability. We've seen him send people away and then bring them back."

"But why me?" said Ricardo.

Rafael took a long drink from a bota bag. "You became too good at your work. Then men began to look at you as the real power here. Don Diego was jealous. I tried to tell you several times to let it appear that he makes the decisions, that he is the real leader."

Ricardo gave his brother a hard look. "I was too busy seeing that this place didn't fall apart."

"El Rancho Grande is in fine condition," Rafael said, implying a double meaning.

Ricardo grinned. "You're right. I didn't listen."

Suddenly, Pedro Gomez walked up to the brothers. "I thought we had seen the last of you," the huge man bellowed. "There's no place around here for a man who loses his guts."

The brothers looked at one another. "Stay out of this, Rafael. This animal is mine," Ricardo said softly.

"Don Diego has awarded me your palomino for killing the Apaches. I want him now," Gomez said in his deep voice.

"Pedro, you are a swine, and you stink of death. Get out of my sight before it's too late," said Ricardo.

Gomez's pig-like eyes were filled with hatred. He growled, and his lips curled back, exposing two rows of rotting teeth. He looked like a rabid grizzly. Pedro pulled a knife from his boot and lumbered forward. Rafael stepped to one side.

Ricardo held his plate in his left hand. He ate another spoonful of beans, chewing slowly, never taking his eyes off Gomez's face.

The huge man was confused and stopped just in front of Ricardo. "I'm going to kill you."

Ricardo's eyes bore into Gomez as he slammed his plate of food into Pedro's face. The fat man yelled and slashed in a semicircle with his knife. Montoya ducked and then buried his fist in the big man's stomach. Pedro's eyes bulged out, and he grabbed his stomach as he doubled over. Ricardo stepped forward and hammered him on the chin. Gomez went down in the dust and dropped his knife. He was breathing heavily as he climbed to his feet and charged Ricardo, grabbing him and attempting to crush him in a bear hug. The two men grunted and growled as they stumbled about.

Ricardo hammered his fist into Pedro's face once, twice, and then a third time before he broke the ox's grip. Gomez was stunned, his eyes glazed and his arms dangling. Ricardo stepped close and hammered the fat man in the belly, then smashed him in the face again and again.

Gomez had been knocked backward against one of the huts and was half-slumped against the wall as he received the intense punishment. His face was raw and bleeding, like a piece of meat.

Rafael ran forward and pulled Ricardo away. "You'll kill him, Ricardo!"

Ricardo was gasping, trying to catch his breath. He put his hands on his hips and took deep breaths as he slowly walked away. The two brothers had gone thirty yards when a shot rang out. It hissed by Montoya's ear.

Ricardo whirled, drew his revolver, and put a bullet through Pedro's forehead. The huge man toppled forward into the dust.

CHAPTER 4

Don Diego Salazar stalked back and forth in front of the men who ran the hacienda. They had assembled at his command and had been subjected to his tirade for the past ten minutes. Most of the men held their sombreros and politely looked at the floor, including Rafael Montoya.

"He insults me, he kills one of my most trusted men, and he leaves. He just *leaves*," Salazar said with emphasis. "No man can leave El Rancho Grande without my permission."

The assembled vaqueros and overseers shifted silently from one foot to another, knowing that Salazar's black temper was reaching its peak. The hacendado's clothing matched his mood, black as always. His jacket was heavily embroidered with silver braid, a red sash wound around his waist. The heels of his highly-polished black boots cracked against the wooden floor as he walked, and he wore a magnificent black sombrero emblazoned with silver.

Salazar's dark eyes glittered as he walked and cursed and berated his subordinates. His small mustache and beard gave him the look of a devil. He stopped in front of Rafael, and his hooded eyes bore into the captain of his bodyguard. Montoya did not look up.

"And you, the brother of that swine! You were there when Gomez was killed, and you did nothing. You let Ricardo walk away. You let him escape!" he yelled. The patron resumed his pacing back and forth in front of his men and again stopped in front of Rafael. "How can I ever trust you again? How can I put my life in your hands again, as I have so many times in the past? Tell me, Rafael."

Rafael raised his eyes, but his face showed no expression. "I have always honored you, Don Diego. Your safety and well-being have always been the most important thing to me. I hope that my past performance in searching out potential dangers and eliminating them has been satisfactory to you. In the future, I will always give you the same loyalty, the same dedication, and the same honor as in the past."

Salazar stared at Montoya, momentarily at a loss for words. His mind raced over what Rafael had said, and he knew it was true that Montoya was the mainstay of his safety. Rafael had the ability to anticipate what Salazar would do, and would make the necessary inspections and placement of vaqueros at vital defensive positions without ever being told. Wherever Don Diego went, Rafael sent men there before him.

The patron loved no man, respected nothing but his own importance, and was only civil when it suited him. But he was intelligent, cunning, calculating, and he knew that he needed a man like Rafael to ensure his protection. Salazar's dilemma made him angry. Should he send Rafael away and surely jeopardize his safety? Or should he keep him in his present position and risk retribution should Ricardo be caught and executed?

"Your performance has been good," said Salazar. "But you know I will hunt Ricardo down and have him shot. There is no way he can betray me and live."

Rafael's placid expression still did not change. "Your protection is my job. The training of men to protect you is my job. The deployment of vaqueros is my job. I know what my jobs are, and I will continue to carry them out if it is your wish," Rafael said quietly.

Salazar was content with the answer. In effect, Rafael was asking to be left alone to carry out his responsibilities, while others could chase the elusive Ricardo. Don Diego was also arrogant enough to believe that his underlings would never attempt to harm him.

"I am a generous man. Is that not so, Rafael?" said Salazar.

"It is," Rafael answered.

"Because I am generous and because I wish you all to know that I continue to think highly of the Montoya family, I will allow Rafael to keep his position." Don Diego announced in a haughty voice. He held out a hand to Rafael, who kissed it.

Salazar dismissed the men. The vaqueros filed quickly out of the room, glad to be away from Salazar's wrath. Rafael stayed behind. As always, he had to be available at a moment's notice. He stared out the window at the rolling hills, trying to bring his anger under control. Montoya knew that staying in his present position was vital. He would be the first to know of all information brought to Don Diego concerning his brother. Rafael was capable of sending a warning quickly. Meanwhile, he would carry out his duties as he always had, in a competent, thorough manner.

***

The Nogales Pass stretched for fourteen miles and was the most direct route between the Gulf of California seaports and central Arizona. People had used the route for over two thousand years. The border town of Nogales was a homogeneous community. The buildings, the life-style, and the people were all similar, no matter which side of the border they lived on. Anglos owned and operated many of the large cattle ranches south of the border, while Mexican land grants were spread over the entire southern section of the Arizona Territory. Gold, silver, and copper mining were booming all along the border, and dozens of American corporations were investing vast sums in the Cananea mines, forty miles to the south.

The United States Army was active at the border, too. The Apaches continued to fight the intrusion of the white men, and many bands refused to live on reservations. Their continual raiding, looting, and killing forced the government to station nearly half the nation's line troops in Arizona.

Ricardo Montoya dismounted in front of Braxton Harvey's law office. He was dressed in heavy broadcloth pants tied with a brown silk sash, and a jacket trimmed in gold braid and embroidery. His palomino's saddle and gear were of a dark, rich leather with extensive gold trim. His leather holster was of the same fine quality, richly hand-tooled, and his .45 had highly polished redwood handle grips.

He opened the outer door and entered the office to find Braxton Harvey bending over the shoulder of one of his law clerks, giving instructions. He was a man of medium height, with curly gray hair, a long face, and light blue eyes. His voice was deep and raspy, and he had the reputation of being a very shrewd lawyer. Ricardo had used Braxton for all of Don Diego's legal work involving mining and cattle, and the two had become good friends and respected one another greatly.

The lawyer poured drinks and handed Ricardo one of his private stock of cigars. "Is this a social visit or business?" asked Harvey.

"Social," said Montoya. "From now on, someone else will be bringing the business to you from Don Diego."

Ricardo spent the next few minutes filling Harvey in on the details. Harvey looked intently at Montoya, amazed at the story.

"Is there any chance this will blow over, and you can go back and live on the ranch?"

"None. I have injured Don Diego's pride and insulted him. He will put a price on my head."

Harvey grunted. "Certainly you exaggerate. People don't kill one another over wounded pride."

"The Mexican culture is much different, Braxton. You are too accustomed to compromise and working out differences in court. In my country, Don Diego is the court."

Harvey's cigar had gone out and he relit it. "Look, I deal with all types of people on both sides of the border. You are the most competent ranch representative or overseer I've ever dealt with. I can get you a well-paying job on either side of the border. Just name it."

"I appreciate your kindness, Braxton. Right now, I need information."

"I'll help you if I can."

"Does any ranch in the area use the initials C and B in their brand or on a crest?"

Harvey sat back in his chair and was lost in thought for a moment. Ricardo watched him closely. "Not that I know of. There's Castro, Castillo, Calderon…Barringer, Billings, Battle, and Burger ranches. None of them use the initials together."

"Were you here twenty-five years ago?" Montoya asked.

"No. I've only been here fifteen years."

"Have you ever heard anything about an ambush of an important family about twenty-five years ago? They had the initials C and B on the coach."

Harvey thought hard and scratched his head. "There have been so many people ambushed and killed by the Indians or outlaws. And ranches have changed hands."

"I understand."

"Wait a minute! I know someone who might remember that far back."

Harvey excused himself, left the office, and gave Ricardo five minutes to himself. When he returned, he had an old man with him. Alf Northrup had been a cowboy, railroader, and miner in the area for fifty years. Now in his eighties, the grizzled old man sat in a rocking chair on the boardwalk every morning and afternoon. Some of the merchants, including Braxton Harvey, saw that the old man had meals and a place to sleep. Alf Northrup loved to drink and talk, and since the store owners didn't supply whiskey to the old man, he did more talking than anything else.

"Say! Whatcha drinkin' there?" he asked Braxton.

Harvey made the introductions and poured Alf a shot of whiskey. The old man tossed off the drink, held out his glass for a refill, and squinted as he studied Ricardo.

"You're a fancy-lookin' Mex," he said in his high scratchy voice.

"It's a pleasure to meet you," said Montoya.

The old man scratched his white beard with his hand, and the second shot disappeared. His eyes sparkled from beneath a wrinkled brow and weather-beaten cheeks as he held out his glass again. Harvey refilled the shot glass.

"Before you drink me dry, I wonder if you can remember back twenty-five years ago," said Braxton.

"I kin remember back fifty years ago. Seems like yesterday," Alf replied.

"Can you remember the ambush of a prominent family?" said Montoya. "Their coach carried the initials C and B. A man, his wife, and little boy died."

Alf tossed the drink down. "You speak good English."

Ricardo looked skeptical and glanced at Harvey. Braxton rose from behind his desk as if to terminate the conversation.

"I remember," Alf said matter-of-factly.

"You do?" Ricardo said in a surprised voice.

The old man held out his glass again. "That's good whiskey, Braxton. We'll have to do this again."

"Would you please tell us, Alf?" said Harvey in a businesslike voice. He filled the old man's glass again.

"Charles Barringer," said Alf. "One of the finest men I ever had the pleasure of knowing."

Ricardo sat upright in his seat, watching the old man intently.

"I was punchin' cows for old Charlie then. His boy, Bob, and his family was ambushed between here and Patagonia. He and his wife and son were all killed. It was a shame. They was such a nice group, not at all like Johnny. When Bob's twin brother, Johnny, took over the spread after old Charlie died, he let me go. Said I was gettin' too old. Johnny's a mean one. He even changed the brand from CB to JB in honor of himself. I'm surprised Victoria let him," Alf said.

"Victoria?" said Ricardo.

"She's John Barringer's mother. A remarkable woman, a pioneer, and true matriarch. The Barringers have one of the largest ranches in the Arizona Territory near Patagonia. I see her occasionally at social gatherings. She moves and talks as if she were a queen," said Harvey.

"She is," said Alf. "Ain't no woman like her 'round here. I felt like workin' for her was an honor." Alf held out his empty glass again.

"One last time," said Harvey. He poured another shot. "Do you have any other questions for Alf?"

Ricardo was silent for a moment before he spoke again. "Do you remember a man with a long scar down his face?" Ricardo traced the path of the scar with his finger on his own face.

"Yup. Scarface, that's what we used to call him...but not to his face. His real name was Ed Graves. Mean, just pure mean. He was foreman of the Barringer spread after Charlie died. Johnny made him foreman. But he ain't there no more. I don't know where he went."

Montoya stared out the window but said nothing. Braxton Harvey studied Ricardo, while Alf Northrup gazed at the liquor bottle on the lawyer's desk.

"Them's sure fancy clothes," said Alf to Ricardo.

Montoya smiled and stood up. "You have been a great help. I appreciate your giving us the time." He handed five dollars to Alf.

The old man smiled. There was a knock on the door, and one of Harvey's clerks entered. "A man is here to see Mr. Montoya," he told Harvey.

Ricardo walked into the main office and over to the vaquero, Jose Moreno. The Mexican cowboy had a sad look on his face. "Rafael sent me. Your father is dead. The funeral is tomorrow. He asks you to be careful," said Moreno.

Ricardo nodded gravely. "Stay here for a day before you start back. Remember, you have never talked to me."

The vaquero acknowledged Montoya's orders and left.

"I must go," Montoya told Harvey. "You have been of great assistance, Braxton. I won't forget it."

The two men shook hands, and Ricardo departed. He turned the information over in his mind as he began the all-night ride back to the Salazar ranch. The trip took him through low mountains and hills and finally leveled out on the high plains that provided thousands of acres of grasslands for the huge cattle herds.

He stopped once to rest the horse and cook some coffee over a small fire. He sat cross-legged and sipped the hot liquid, gazing into the fire. *Who am I?* He thought. *Is my name Barringer? Do I really want to know?*

He finished the second cup, stretched his long frame, yawned, and climbed back into the saddle. He patted his horse, Oro, and they continued the trip back to El Rancho Grande. Daylight was just breaking over the eastern mountains as he entered the hill country surrounding the ranch headquarters. The hills took on a blue-green hue in the early light, and the streams winding through the valleys sparkled. Gold, black, and green plots of land spread out among the hills, creating a rich patchwork-quilt effect.

Ricardo stayed off the main trails and picked his way through the back country until he was above the small, white church where he knew the ceremony would take place. He unsaddled the palomino, slipped on his poncho, and sat against a large tree. Ricardo was asleep within minutes.

The ringing of the church bells awoke him. He watched as the families of peons and vaqueros filed into the church. When it was full, the ranch families gathered outside. After the service, the procession moved to the cemetery. Montoya sat on his horse on top of the hill adjacent to the graveyard, and all the families saw him. As they sang hymns, their eyes gradually moved to Ricardo until the congregation of more than two hundred men, women, and children were all gazing at him. The priest turned his head, recognized Ricardo, and said a silent prayer.

Gustavo Montoya was laid to rest, and his grave was covered with a mound of brilliant flowers. The headstone was engraved with his name and a simple message: "A friend to all."

After the mourners had departed, Ricardo rode down to his father's grave. He knelt there and prayed.

"You are my father, and I'll always love you," he said quietly. "It makes no difference what you told me. I'll always remember your goodness and will try to honor you, Father."

Ricardo stood up, replaced his sombrero, and wiped his eyes. In the distance he saw a lone figure appear at the end of the valley and ride toward him. Rafael Montoya pulled his horse up, dismounted, and the two men embraced.

After sharing their grief, Rafael changed the subject. "There is something else you should know."

"What is it?"

"The patron had a visitor, Alfredo Villalobos."

"The one known as El Lobo, the wolf?"

"Yes. The hired killer. His headquarters is in Hermosillo," said Rafael. "He came for payment in advance."

"Am I the target?"

"I took the liberty of listening at the wall. Don Carlos Bustamante is the prime target. You are secondary. El Lobo leaves today for the Bustamante rancho."

"But why?"

"Don Carlos will not sell the disputed pasturelands. Don Diego needs them badly for his new herds. He must fatten them up before turning them over to the Yankees," said Rafael.

"Does he really think he can get away with it?"

"Who knows? Bustamante has only one child, a daughter, as you well know. Don Diego may believe that she will not go against him when he moves in on the pastures. Something else was strange," said Rafael.

"What?"

"El Lobo was instructed to face Don Carlos and tell him that Don Diego sends his regards, and then kill him."

CHAPTER 5

From his hiding place in a stand of walnut trees, Alfredo Villalobos watched the vaqueros round up the cattle in the valley below him. He recognized the patron, Don Carlos Bustamante, by his dignified richness of clothing and magnificent white horse. Don Carlos was slightly separated from the moving herd.

Villalobos had a dark, oval face and hooded, close-set eyes. Below his large, flat nose were a tiny mustache and small mouth, dwarfed by a large square chin. He was an ugly man with a deceptively sleepy appearance. Villalobos had gained a well-deserved reputation as a hired killer, and had picked up the nickname el lobo solitario, "the lone wolf."

He had been paid handsomely to put an end to Don Carlos, and was waiting for an opportunity to catch the patron away from his vaqueros. That moment was at hand. Bustamante rode back up the valley to determine if any stragglers had been missed.

El Lobo mounted his horse and quickly rode down the hill to intercept Don Carlos. As he reached the flat grasslands, another figure spurred his mount from the trees on the hill directly above Bustamante. Both figures converged on Don Carlos at the same time.

The second rider reached Bustamante before El Lobo did. Don Carlos was confused as he looked from one man to the other. Bustamante wore a revolver, but he was not a fast draw or good shot. He sensed something was wrong by the way the two men eyed each other.

"Lobo," said Ricardo Montoya. "I know why you're here."

"Who are you?" asked Villalobos.

"I'm the second man you're supposed to kill. Ricardo Montoya is my name."

El Lobo's hooded eyes opened slightly. "This will save me much time and trouble," he said, leering. Then he turned to Bustamante. "Don Carlos, I bring you the compliments of Don Diego Salazar."

***

Bustamante sensed what was about to happen, but he couldn't believe the scene as it unfolded before him. Both men drew their revolvers and fired almost simultaneously at one another. Villalobos was struck in the chest, threw his arms back, and toppled over the rear of his horse. Montoya was hit in the left side. He dropped his revolver, grabbed the saddle horn, and slid to the ground, where he rolled onto his back.

"My God," Bustamante whispered.

The patron jumped out of the saddle and rushed to Montoya's side. Ricardo was barely conscious and bleeding badly. The gunfire had brought two of Bustamante's vaqueros riding up at top speed.

"Get the wagon!" Bustamante yelled.

They worked on Montoya's wound and were finally able to stop the bleeding. Ricardo's face was white and his breathing was labored. The landowner walked over to Villalobos. The dead man's unseeing eyes looked skyward, and a surprised expression was captured on his face. Don Carlos shook his head from side to side, then hurriedly walked back to Ricardo.

"What happened?" one of the cowboys asked.

"The dead one was hired to kill me," said Bustamante. "Montoya intercepted him, and they shot each other right in front of me. What do you think about Ricardo's wound?"

The small cowboy shrugged his shoulders. "The bullet went through, but it will depend on how much blood he has lost and if it hit any vital organs."

It took four hours to transport Ricardo back to the Bustamante ranch. His wounds were cleaned and bandaged, and he was left to sleep in one of the spare bedrooms.

**

Maria Bustamante sat in a large chair next to the bed and took the first watch, gazing at his face. His features had softened in his unconscious state. The creases were relaxed around the eyes and down the sides of his face. His high forehead, smooth cheeks, and broad chin were accented by a strong nose, dark eyebrows, and mustache. *A handsome man*, she thought, *almost pretty*. But, his life was filled with violence. *Do I enter into a passionate, tempestuous relationship with Ricardo and let my heart overrule common sense, or do I think rationally about his dangerous lifestyle, knowing that he could be killed at any moment? Is he the man for me, or do I want a normal man who displays safety above valor?*

Ricardo groaned, and his eyes fluttered open. He stared at the ceiling, not seeming to know where he was. His eyes moved until he could see Maria, and the recollection of what had occurred made itself known in his eyes.

"Lobo…." he croaked.

"Please don't try to talk, Ricardo. The other man is dead, but my father was not injured. You're wounded in the side," she told him as she bent over the bed.

Montoya didn't say anything. He looked at her for a few moments and then closed his eyes and drifted off.

***

Maria and the other ranch women took turns feeding Montoya during the next two days. His improvement was rapid. On the fourth day, he and Don Carlos had a brief conversation.

"I'm so glad you are recovering. You've saved my life twice. There's no way to repay you except to say that my ranch is yours. After you have recovered, I would like you to stay," the good-natured rancher said.

"Thank you," said Ricardo.

"Now, can you tell me what happened?" Don Carlos asked.

"To put it briefly, Don Diego hired El Lobo to kill you. I think it was because of your conflict over the pastureland. He was also hired to kill me," said Montoya.

Don Carlos got up from the chair next to the bed and walked to the small window. "The man must be crazy."

"As his holdings became bigger and he became more powerful and influential, he began to change," said Montoya. "Money and absolute power corrupted him. He just wants more and more and will tolerate no interference from anyone."

Bustamante turned and inspected Montoya. "What would you recommend I do now?"

Ricardo outlined his ideas. Don Carlos left a few minutes later, and Ricardo fell asleep. He dreamed he was riding Oro across the grasslands, feeling the muscles and the movement of the big animal under him. He awoke with a smile on his face. Maria Bustamante was studying him. Her expression suddenly changed from one of pleasure to guarded appraisal once she realized he was awake, as if he could read her thoughts. They observed one another for a moment.

"I, like my father, wish to thank—" she began, but Ricardo cut her off.

"I understand," said Montoya.

"Is there anything I can get you?" she asked.

"Nothing."

"Do you want me to leave?" she said.

Ricardo did not answer. Maria rose and moved toward the door.

"I know you don't approve of me. Being here is not my idea," he said.

She stopped and turned around. "I don't mean to give you that impression," she said quietly. Concern was mirrored in her eyes.

Ricardo was tired, his side ached, and he didn't want to play games. He felt defeated and frustrated in his desire to win her approval and love. Ricardo had a strong yearning to be with her, but his emotions were in turmoil over her condemnation of his lifestyle. He stared at her, knowing he was not up to arguing about justice or his way of living.

Her dark eyes indicated she was offended, but Ricardo had shifted his gaze to the window and did not see her reaction. She opened the door and left quietly.

During the next few weeks, Montoya made a rapid recovery. His wound healed fast, his strength returned, and he was riding again within a month of the shoot-out. Bustamante continued to ask Ricardo for advice about the running of his rancho, the deployment of vaqueros for ranching purposes, the layout of the buildings surrounding the headquarters, and about the cattle market. Don Carlos had only about one-sixth the number of men that Don Diego could call upon, and a much smaller ranch. Bustamante did most of the overseeing himself and was quick to seek the advice of the man who had built his competitor's ranch into an empire.

Ricardo recommended dispersing the cattle to reduce the chances of over-grazing, establishing line camps to oversee the herds, clearing much of the timber around the ranch house and its outbuildings as a precaution against Indian attack, and building peons' houses in a tight cluster around the main headquarters.

Ricardo admired Don Carlos's quick wit, decency, sense of dignity, and his kindness to the peons and vaqueros. Bustamante, in turn, began to look upon Montoya as a son.

One day the two men were sitting down to eat lunch after a morning of branding and counting cows prior to the cattle drive north to the Arizona Territory.

"How much training have the peons had in firearms?" Ricardo asked.

"None," said Bustamante.

"You have a substantial storehouse of revolvers and rifles. In case of a major Apache attack, you could double your firepower by using the peons." Don Carlos thought about it for a moment. "You're right."

"It's simply a matter of giving them the instruction and setting up a schedule for repeating their training each year. I'll be glad to do it," said Montoya.

Two days later, nearly fifty peons were lined up in a meadow as Ricardo explained the use of a variety of firearms, including the Henry and Winchester .44 repeating rifles. Before letting them fire bullets, he taught them how to position their hands and arms, how to sight a target, and how to steady the firearms. Then he let them pull the triggers on empty guns. This went on for more than an hour, and then he instructed them in loading weapons. White clay bricks were set up as targets. Don Carlos Bustamante paced the ground behind the shooting range, wondering how the experiment would work.

"Ready, aim, fire!" Ricardo yelled.

The ensuing fusillade of gunfire resulted in a deafening roar throughout the clearing. Peons were thrown backward by the kick from the gun butts; others dropped their weapons and grabbed their ears. Two of them ran. The entire shooting area was shrouded in smoke created by the black gunpowder.

Don Carlos had stopped in his tracks and looked horrified. His eyes were wide, and his mouth dropped open as he surveyed the tangled mass of men and weapons. Bustamante turned his head and looked at Montoya. Ricardo's smile became a grin, and then he began laughing. The landowner was dumbfounded for a moment, and then he started laughing. They walked toward one another.

"Was this your idea of a joke?" Don Carlos asked as tears ran down his cheeks.

"I knew this would happen. It always does the first time," said Ricardo. "You have to get them over their initial fright involving noise. Each time it gets better."

"If nothing else, they'd certainly scare the Apaches," Bustamante said.

During the next two hours, Ricardo took five peons at a time and gave individual instruction. The other workers stood behind and watched as their companions fired the rifles. Toward the end of the day, the majority of the peons were able to come close to the targets.

The rifle training went on for a week until most of the men could load and fire their weapons without help. Many of the vaqueros were skilled in the use of rifles, but Montoya made them all take the same practice.

Bustamante had a variety of side arms, including .36 caliber navy Colts, Remington .44's, and a Starr double-action army .44. A few of the vaqueros had the new Colt .45's, but the majority used the old cap-and-ball firearms. None of the revolvers were very accurate at over sixty feet, so Ricardo taught the peons how to load the guns and had them shoot at man-sized targets twenty feet away.

"The idea is to keep your enemies at long range with the rifles. You only use the revolvers in close combat," he emphasized.

Further training was postponed for a week until a fresh supply of lead, powder, percussion caps, and cartridges arrived. During the final day of training, Ricardo and Don Carlos stood together watching the shooting.

"They'll be able to defend themselves now," said Ricardo.

"It surprises me that they learned so fast," said Don Carlos.

"They have wives and children, and the Apaches won't stay on the reservations forever."

"Did you train Salazar's peons?"

"No. He didn't trust too many armed men around him."

Don Carlos smiled. "I wonder what he thinks of the presents we sent him."

Villalobos's boots and revolver had been packaged and sent to Don Diego, along with the message that Don Carlos demanded satisfaction. The note said: *Your treachery and deceit is beyond comprehension. I have taken the opportunity to notify your neighboring ranchers so they may guard against assassins sent by you.*

Being challenged to a personal duel, in addition to being exposed before his neighbors, would infuriate Salazar, yet it would make him wary of trying his scheme a second time.

Ricardo grinned as he thought about Salazar. "He paces back and forth when he's upset. By now, he's probably worn out the rugs in his office."

Don Carlos laughed.

***

Maria joined the two men for lunch on the patio. Ricardo and Maria had successfully avoided being alone together during the past weeks. When Don Carlos was present, they were polite to each other but did not talk at length on any subject. Bustamante noticed their strangely superficial behavior and was puzzled. In the middle of the meal, he excused himself and went to speak briefly with a vaquero. The silence grew between Maria and Ricardo.

"When will the cattle drive depart?" she finally asked.

"Next week. Will that be soon enough?" he said in an even voice.

"I was just asking to make conversation," Maria said softly.

Ricardo inspected the raven-haired woman. She returned his gaze in a frank manner.

"I know you think I'm partially responsible for the danger your father is in. I may be, but these are violent times," he said firmly.

"And you're a violent man."

"One does what one has to do."

"This is the life you choose," she pointed out.

"You know nothing about my life. Nothing about what or who I am. You make judgments based on little knowledge and a lot of speculation," he emphasized. "I saved your life and I saved your father's life twice. That should tell you something about the land we live in."

"We do appreciate what you have done for us. I realize we wouldn't be alive without your help."

"You miss the point. Circumstances dictate what action has to be taken in a frontier with little or no law," Ricardo stated.

She continued to look at him. No one had ever spoken to her in that tone of voice except her nanny and her mother when she was a small girl. Maria saw before her a man who was tough, unyielding, and sometimes uncompromising. She was repulsed by his savage attitude, yet strangely drawn to him at the same time.

Montoya suddenly seemed to realize he had overstepped the bounds of propriety. "I'm sorry. I had no right to say those things to you."

He rose and excused himself.

"Wait!" she said in a strained voice. "Don't go." Tears came to her eyes. Emotional turmoil forced frustration and passion to collide, leaving her vulnerable and yearning for a man she knew was wrong for her. Ricardo stood still. She was almost pleading as she looked at him. "I didn't realize my approval meant that much to you," she said.

He took a deep breath. "It does."

"Then, let's try to treat each other better, please."

***

Something else was troubling Ricardo. He had made up his mind on a course of action. This was as good a time as any to tell them.

After Don Carlos had returned, Ricardo spoke up. "I won't be coming back with you after the cattle drive."

The hurt showed immediately on Don Carlos's face. Maria looked stunned. Ricardo plunged into the story about what his father had told him before he died. He also explained about his trip to Nogales and what he had learned about the Barringers.

Bustamante looked dumbfounded. "You are a Mexican as surely as I am."

"The stories from my father and the old man in Nogales coincide. There are many questions I must find answers to," Ricardo explained.

Don Carlos stroked his white beard. "Your soul must be heavy," he said.

***

Ricardo lay in bed unable to sleep that night. He got up, dressed, and wandered out into the patio garden. While he stood looking at the moon and stars, inhaling the cool night air, he heard a rustle of clothing behind him and turned quickly. Maria stood there, pale in the moonlight. She ran into his arms, and her fingers dug into him. He kissed her long and passionately, and she responded with spontaneous excitement.

LEE BISHOP

CHAPTER 6

Don Carlos Bustamante made his most successful sale of beef yet to the United States Army in the Arizona Territory, thanks in part to Montoya's connections and experience north of the border. For two days, the crew gambled, partied, and drank the saloons dry before Don Carlos was ready to leave for the long trip back to his ranch.

The rancher postponed his departure from Nogales until it was no longer reasonable to stay. The silver-haired rancher stood on the boardwalk outside the hotel and talked with Ricardo. His eyes pleaded with Montoya.

"Is there anything I can say that will change your mind? You have become like a son to me. I fear I will not see you again should you leave now," Don Carlos said.

Ricardo had begun to feel a strong attachment to the old man with the silver beard and laughing eyes. But Montoya was not accustomed to a genuine show of affection and felt ill at ease.

"I will be back to see you. Count on it," he assured the rancher.

"Is it so important to find out?" Don Carlos asked quietly.

Montoya nodded. "My life is very confused. Perhaps I can only straighten it out by starting at the beginning. I know I must try."

The two men looked at each other, and an understanding passed between them.

Don Carlos suddenly smiled, and then laughed. "Well, go then, so you can come back soon!"

"One last thing," said Ricardo. "I have only the highest regard and respect for your daughter."

"I believe it is her intention to wait," said Bustamante. "But don't take too long. She is twenty and well on her way to being an old maid."

Both men laughed. Don Carlos grabbed Ricardo in a bear hug and pounded him on the back. He then mounted his horse and rode down the street at the head of his vaqueros.

Ricardo felt a pang of regret as he watched Bustamante depart. Oro was saddled and waiting for Montoya when he reached the stable. The story of his exploits in fighting the Apaches, his blood feud with Salazar, the killing of El Lobo, and the clash with *banditos* had made him somewhat of a celebrity here. Now, as he rode Oro through the main Mexican section of Nogales, the peons came to their doors and windows to watch him pass. They talked excitedly to one another and kept their eyes on him until he was out of sight.

Montoya headed northeast along the trail toward Patagonia. He passed cowboys, coaches, and wagons on the busy route between the burgeoning mining town and the border city. The range land was golden and almost free of trees in some areas between the low-lying mountain ranges. As the road climbed higher, it traveled along a stream that wound its way through stands of trees.

As Ricardo traveled farther north, the difference in clothing between what the Yankee cowboy and the vaquero wore became more pronounced. Most of the cowboys in the Arizona Territory wore close-fitting woolen pants or jeans with simple dark-colored flannel shirts. High-crowned, wide-brimmed Stetsons, high-heeled cowboy boots, and bright bandannas were common.

Ricardo looked out of place in his expensive south-of-the-border clothing. His beautifully decorated saddle was far different from the plain, dark leather of the average cowboy's rig. He received many hard, scrutinizing looks from the cattlemen and common cowboys who passed him.

Soon Ricardo entered Patagonia and rode down the dusty main street. He looked the town over in a matter of minutes and then continued on the trail north. By now he was in the mile-high, rolling country that was becoming famous for its huge cattle herds. Montoya rode for another half hour before he began to see the JB brand on the cattle.

Following the directions he had been given, Ricardo took a trail to the left until he could make out the ranch house in the distance. He walked Oro up a small hill and into some trees, noting that the ranch house, its adjoining buildings, and numerous corrals were out in the open, making a successful Indian attack unlikely. A coach was driven out of one of the barns, and a half dozen riders gathered in front of the huge home. A figure in a long, dark dress got into the coach.

Montoya mounted his horse and backtracked until he reached the main road again and followed it until he came to a ford in the stream. Fifteen minutes later the coach and men came into sight. A cowboy rode on each side, and the remaining four men trailed along behind. Ricardo let his horse drink on the opposite side of the stream.

***

The coach thundered down the embankment and slowed as it hit the water. Montoya looked directly into the coach at the elderly woman inside. Her blue eyes held his for an instant and looked away, then snapped back. She leaned over to get a better look out the window and yelled, "Stop the coach!" The driver pulled the two coach horses to a halt on the other side of the stream opposite Ricardo.

Victoria Barringer held onto the door sill and stared at Montoya. Her eyes were riveted on the tall Mexican, who removed his sombrero and nodded to her in a courteous manner. Victoria's eyes moved slowly over all of his features, including his curly black hair.

My God, she thought, *he looks identical to my husband when we were first married.*

Her gaze moved over his clothing and then back to his face. A less confident woman would not have been so obvious with her intent to closely examine the man in front of her. But, Victoria was not demure and modesty seldom crossed her mind.

Although over seventy, the thin woman had maintained much of her earlier beauty. She had magnificent, penetrating blue eyes that engulfed whatever she looked at. Her face was oval, almost fragile, accented by high cheekbones and a straight nose. Victoria's mouth was set firmly as she inspected Ricardo.

One of the cowboys rode up and tipped his hat. "Anything wrong, Mrs. Barringer?"

"Nothing, thank you," she said in a perfectly articulated voice. "Tell the driver to continue."

***

Ricardo stood quietly as the coach thundered away. He waited for a few minutes, then mounted and rode after the coach. When he reached Patagonia, he stabled Oro and had his saddle locked away. Then he checked into the large, two-story hotel in the center of town. He listened to the conversation in the ornately decorated lobby.

"Victoria Barringer is here for the wedding," a large woman in a dark dress said to another matronly-looking lady. "Of course, she has the governor's suite in the back of the hotel."

Montoya walked down the hall to the rear of the hotel and stepped out in back. A balcony projected outward from one corner of the second floor, which he assumed was the governor's suite. He went to the barbershop for a trim and shave and then to the bath house. Afterward, Ricardo returned to his room and lay down on the bed to think. He rested until dinnertime and then walked to the dining room.

The room was bathed in light from a huge assortment of chandeliers and lanterns. The carpeting was rich in color, and the tables were covered in fine linen. Sterling silver and imported crystal reflected the bright lights. The majority of men and women in these elegant surroundings were dressed in suits and expensive dresses. The hotel establishment immediately recognized Montoya as being a member of the landed gentry from Mexico, and had appreciated his gold payment in advance for the room. His clothing contrasted sharply with the rather subdued suits of the local merchants and ranchers.

But, as he walked in long strides to his table, his demeanor was unmistakably that of a leader and one who held a high position in society. Many of the women gave quick admiring glances to Montoya, attracted by his dignified air and handsome physique.

Victoria Barringer regarded Montoya discreetly as he seated himself and began to read the menu. She was sitting at the head of the largest table in the room and was the object of a great deal of attention. While studying Ricardo, she still kept up with the conversation at the table. Her every movement was graceful, and she maintained a regal bearing. When she smiled, her beautiful white teeth were dazzling.

Montoya was easily able to study the matriarch because he was alone at his table. Victoria Barringer was wearing a dark blue velvet dress, trimmed in white silk. Several strings of pearls encircled her neck. She wore matching earrings, a diamond-and-pearl bracelet, and sparkling diamond rings. Her hair was piled high on her head, as current fashion dictated. Ricardo decided that her dignity and grace were complemented by a certain aloofness, which only added to her elegance.

Their eyes met several times, and Ricardo knew that she was studying him just as he was scrutinizing her. As she nodded and listened to the conversation swirling around her, Victoria's eyes would suddenly rise now and then to inspect Montoya. Then they would return quickly to her companions. From bits and pieces of their conversation, Ricardo knew they were going to attend a house party following the dinner.

After finishing his meal, he walked to a nearby gambling casino. An hour later, he cashed in his chips and walked back to the hotel. He walked to the rear of the building and quickly scaled a fire-escape ladder. One of the windows was open, and he easily climbed from the balcony into the bedroom of the governor's suite and opened the drapes, which led into the parlor. The smell of expensive perfume was strong.

***

An hour later, Victoria Barringer let herself into her suite and dropped her shawl on a chair. She looked at herself in the wall mirror and smiled. She was pleased with the evening's events, which included her selection of a wife for her grandson. Young William Barringer didn't know it yet, but she had decided that he would marry Agatha Hale, the daughter of a local mine owner. The young woman was pretty, of average intelligence, and looked as if she would be a good breeder, Victoria believed.

The matriarch walked over to the drapes and thrust them aside. She gave a startled cry as the material parted, and before her stood the tall Mexican stranger she had seen at dinner. Victoria quickly regained her composure.

"Do you mind telling me the meaning of this?" she asked sharply.

"I'm not here to harm you. I need to talk with you, and privately," Ricardo explained.

Her eyes moved up and down the man in front of her. *It can't be*, she thought. "What is so important that you must break into my room?"

"I have information about your son Robert's death many years ago."

Victoria's eyes were riveted upon Ricardo. "Surely you jest!"

"I will tell you what I was told. May we sit down?" he asked.

She contemplated what he'd said and then indicated with her hand the couch and chair at one side of the room. She seated herself with unpretentious dignity.

"Now go ahead," she said quietly.

"There was a witness to the killing of your son's family."

"No man ever came forward before," she said firmly.

"My father was camped near the site. He heard the shooting and ran to investigate, but he was unarmed. Assassins did it and made it look like a robbery," said Ricardo.

Victoria's blue eyes blazed. "Rubbish! Pure rubbish!"

"It's true. My father told me as he was dying. He was the kind of man who never lied."

She jumped to her feet. "I don't wish to hear any more of this absurd story."

Ricardo's eyes bored into her. "You sound as if you don't want to know the truth."

"I know nothing about you, and I'm not interested in continuing this preposterous dialogue."

Montoya was angry. "You will listen. Now sit down!" he said firmly. He continued without waiting for a reply. "The boy was never found, was he? What was his name?"

Victoria's expression suddenly froze. "James," she whispered.

"My father found where the woman had hidden the boy in the rocks before she was killed. It may have been wrong, but he took the boy and raised him as his own son. Partly to protect him from another attempt on his life."

Victoria had a pained look on her face as she stared at Ricardo. "What are you trying to tell me?" she asked.

"I am that boy," he said quietly.

Tears suddenly appeared in the corners of Victoria Barringer's eyes. But she maintained her poise.

"Really?" she said in a voice that cracked, and her body trembled slightly.

"I have no way of proving what I say," said Montoya. "It's just that my father never lied to me in all his life. I don't think he would do so on his deathbed."

She took a deep breath. "There is one way to verify your story."

Ricardo's face registered surprise. "How?"

She moved gracefully across the few feet that separated them. "Unbutton your shirt," she ordered in a surprisingly strong voice.

Their eyes locked, and his lit up as he suddenly seemed to realize what she meant. He did as she instructed, and she pulled the shirt apart and gazed at the triangular birthmark below his heart.

Victoria dropped her head while she composed herself. When she raised her head, she was smiling.

"Well now, a gift from heaven," she said quietly, and patted his chest. "Wait until John hears that he has a nephew."

"You mean my...uncle," he said, as if unwilling to make the pronouncement.

"Exactly," she said, and her eyes gleamed. She encircled Ricardo's arm with hers. "Come sit beside me, James. We have much to discuss." She flashed him a bright smile.

"My name is Ricardo," he said, and grinned.

They looked into each other's eyes and the bond seemed instant.

"Not anymore, Grandson. Not anymore. You're back after twenty-six years."

***

They talked for another hour. After Ricardo went back to his room, he had a difficult time falling asleep.

The following morning he reluctantly arose to a repeated knocking on the door. He opened it and was confronted by a short cowboy, who looked at him with distrust.

"Mrs. Barringer says she'd like to have breadfas' with ya in an hour," the cowhand stated.

Montoya said he would be down after washing up. An hour later he knocked on the door of the governor's suite. A man dressed in a dark suit opened the door and scrutinized Ricardo as he stepped aside. Victoria Barringer stood in the center of the room with three other well-dressed men.

"Ah. There you are, James," said Victoria. She glided across the floor, hooked her arm through Ricardo's, and led him over to the other men.

"I would like you to meet my grandson, James," she said smoothly.

Ricardo shook hands with the men as Victoria named them. Among the group was Bob Giddings, the most prominent banker in the community; Kevin Johnson, a mine owner; Ralph Bertram, owner of both the hotel and the largest mercantile store in Patagonia; and Harry Palmer, the Barringers' lawyer. Palmer was an older, gray-haired man, known for his shrewd business dealings and contractual expertise. He hung back slightly from the group to appraise Montoya. He was impressed by the man's size, obvious power, and straightforward manner.

Palmer was the only man in the room who had known Charles Barringer when he was alive. He noted that if Ricardo would shave his mustache and have his hair cut shorter, he would closely resemble the old cattle baron. There was no mistaking the ancestry.

Victoria had already briefed the men on Ricardo's background, his fall from grace as Salazar's adviser, and his recent discovery of his true identity. She was brilliantly charming as she guided the conversation toward her own ends.

As usual, Victoria held center stage with a straightforward, perfectly timed, and articulated delivery of speech that left the businessmen shaking their heads in agreement. She wore a dark green dress set off by an awesome array of emerald jewelry.

"Now, to get down to business, gentlemen," she said as they finished a late breakfast. "I wanted you all to meet James so you can verify that I legally recognize him to be a legitimate heir to the Barringer holdings."

The banker, Giddings, choked on his coffee and turned red. A slight smile passed over Palmer's lips. Ricardo looked surprised, as did the other men.

"Have you talked this over with John?" asked a worried Giddings.

"There's no need. Legally, I control the Barringer empire, and I am satisfied that this man is my grandson," she said in a charming voice.

She looked from one man to another. Her smile was dazzling, but her eyes kept their calculating look.

"I beg your pardon, Mrs. Barringer, but there's bound to be trouble," said Giddings, a typically cautious and unimaginative banker.

"I'll take care of John," Victoria said firmly.

Ricardo spoke up. "I am not here to claim anything...Grandmother. I don't even know that I will stay."

"You will," she said brightly. "Before we leave for the ranch today, Harry, I want you to draw up the necessary codicil to my will naming Ricardo as an heir with equal rights to those of John and his son, William."

There was an uncomfortable silence around the table.

"And, gentlemen, you will all sign it as witnesses," she said in her smooth voice.

None of the men uttered a sound. Their gazes moved back and forth from Victoria to James.

"Don't look so dumbfounded. I'm satisfied that he is my grandson. John will look at James from a different perspective when he understands that James is a legitimate heir to the Barringer Ranch and our other holdings. What I'm attempting to do is head off any immediate problems," she told the assembled men.

The men looked at one another but said nothing.

"Good," she said happily. "Now that that's decided and business is out of the way, I'm sure there are many questions you have for James."

Victoria Barringer sat back in her chair like a queen on her throne. As the businessmen questioned Ricardo, she toyed with a fan. But her eyes betrayed that her mind was appraising, digesting, analyzing, and making future plans.

From time to time, Ricardo glanced at his grandmother as he talked and answered questions concerning his past. Each time he looked into her penetrating blue eyes, he felt as if she were dissecting him.

CHAPTER 7

The coach bumped, rattled, and swayed along the dirt road leading up to the Barringer ranch house. Victoria and Ricardo sat opposite each other on black leather seats and talked about a wide range of subjects during their return to the ranch.

"Do the Apaches bother you much?" Ricardo asked.

"Not much during the past ten years. It has been my philosophy to let them have a cow or two when they need beef. It's simply easier to live with them and give up some cattle than it is to fight them and expend both money and energy trying to corral the elusive creatures," she said, smiling.

"On the Salazar ranch it was a matter of pride of ownership," he said.

Victoria's eyes appraised Ricardo. "Cattle are to be used, not worshiped. They are merely a tool."

"How large are the holdings?"

"Nearly eight hundred thousand acres and growing," said Victoria in a matter-of-fact voice. "It is my goal to see that the Barringer holdings become the largest cattle empire in the Southwest."

"You and Don Diego Salazar have a lot in common, Grandmother."

"Probably we would understand one another," she said, and her eyes sparkled. "By the way, you won't like John when you meet him. He's not the likable sort. But he is a hard worker. And he has managed to carry on where his father left off. He's been in Tucson on business, but he should be getting back about now."

Montoya was silent for a few moments and stared out the window. His gaze returned to his grandmother. "What was my father like?"

She smiled. "He was big, like you, intelligent, and tough. He always beat John when the two of them would fight. Robert had a good sense of humor and was the obvious choice to take over the ranch. Your mother was a bright, intelligent girl. I have missed them both very much."

"They were killed by white men," he said.

"I find that hard to believe," said Victoria.

Her eyes were mere slits, and it was impossible for Montoya to read her thoughts. Ricardo's attention suddenly shifted to the ranch house as they approached the huge mansion on the hill surrounded by a variety of miscellaneous buildings.

Victoria was watching Ricardo as he studied the layout.

"Magnificent, isn't it?" she said. "Charles built it, and it is still the finest home in the territory."

Victoria explained that the house resembled a French colonial mansion. The huge rectangular structure was two stories high and had a full basement. The outer walls were made of brick that had been fired in kilns built on the property. A pillared veranda ran around all four sides of the home, providing shade for the windows and a comfortable breezy place to sit and relax.

The outside of the veranda was a façade of crisscrossing patterns of California redwood, with delicate colonnettes extending to the roof. A long hallway ran down the center of the forty-room house, dividing various bedrooms, a study, library, living room, and offices. At the northern end of the house were the kitchen and storage rooms. Every major room had its own fireplace. Charles Barringer had decreed that all people would be comfortable and warm while under his roof.

The second floor belonged entirely to Victoria. It consisted of her bedroom, a lavishly decorated parlor, sewing room, dining room, and quarters for two maids who waited on Mrs. Barringer day and night.

There were three large barns on the property, a blacksmith's shop, a machine shop, five other service buildings, four bunk houses, and a shop for manufacturing harnesses and other leather goods. Near the house were rose gardens, and half a mile away stood large orchards of fruit trees, and vegetable and melon gardens.

The coach pulled to a halt in front of one of the massive staircases climbing to the veranda. Victoria was helped from the carriage and was kissed by a tall, gangly youth, who looked to be about twenty years old. She patted him on the cheek.

"William, I want you to meet James, a cousin you didn't know you had," said Victoria.

The tall youth looked confused. "What?" he said.

"Never mind, dear, just follow me into the house," she said.

William Barringer had a thin body, a long face, and sensitive brown eyes. He was unable to mask his feelings and emotions, and a skeptical, almost fearful look crossed his face. Ricardo shook hands with the young man and tried to put him at ease.

Once inside the living room, Victoria sat down in a large armchair. She was both charming and incisive as she informed William about Ricardo.

The youth looked from his grandmother to Ricardo and back again. His mouth hung open. "Does Father know?"

"Not yet," said Victoria, and she smiled. "It should be an interesting surprise."

William look worried. "Grandmother, he isn't going to like it."

Her eyes flashed. "I'm going to enjoy it."

Ricardo stood to one side watching the two talk. He stood in a relaxed manner with his thumbs hooked over his gun belt. *The boy's had all the fight kicked out of him*, Ricardo thought.

"I suppose you'd like to see some pictures of your family," Victoria said, turning to Ricardo.

"Yes, I would."

She stood up, walked to a large desk, and took an album from one of the bottom drawers. She placed it on a table, opened it, and took out several photos. First, she handed Ricardo a wedding picture showing his father and mother in their early twenties. He could see similarities between himself and the man smiling in the picture. What moved him most was the photo of his mother, Jane, a dark-haired beauty whose soft features and smiling eyes revealed what a charming lady she must have been. He studied it for several moments while the Barringers watched him.

"Was she as nice as she looked?"

"Positively enchanting," Victoria replied, studying him. "It's common not to remember anything about your early life," she said, reading his mind. He glanced up at her and then back down at the photos.

When they heard several horses approaching the house, William walked to the window and looked out.

"It's Father!" the young man exclaimed. He walked from the room without saying another word.

Victoria touched her fingertips together as she sat in the chair and gave Ricardo a cunning look. "Nice boy, but John's been too hard on him."

Montoya thought the young man looked like a whipped pup.

***

The front door burst open and heavy footsteps echoed in the hallway. A bearlike man walked into the room and looked with distaste at Montoya and his grandmother.

John Barringer had a huge head and a large, flat face with a square chin. His mustache was a wide expanse of black below a big nose, and his bushy eyebrows came together above it. His eyes were large and almost black. Overall, his appearance was one of barely contained hostility. He was half a head shorter than Montoya, but his body was big and muscular.

"John, I want you to meet James Barringer, your late brother's son, who survived that ambush many years ago. However, I don't think you'll want to call him nephew," said Victoria in her silky, polished voice.

John looked at Ricardo and then back at his mother. "I'm in no mood for jokes," he said in a deep booming voice.

"It's not meant as one," said Victoria in a calculating tone of voice. "It seems that James was not killed along with the rest of his family. He was found by a man who witnessed the ambush, and was raised in Mexico as his son."

Ricardo studied Barringer intently. John turned his massive head slowly and inspected Montoya.

"The resemblance to your father is remarkable, isn't it?" said Victoria.

"This is all a bunch of bull, and I want you off this ranch," said John.

Victoria was smiling now. "Johnny, he has the birthmark under his heart to prove who he is."

"I don't want to hear any more of this!" John shouted.

Victoria's eyes gleamed. "I had James written into the will. When I'm gone, he's to share with you and your son."

"I don't accept any of this," said Barringer. "This is crazy!" He advanced on Ricardo. "Let's see that birthmark, Mex."

Montoya straightened up, and his gaze bore into Barringer. "I wouldn't do that if I were you."

Barringer stopped advancing when he recognized that Montoya could not be intimidated. Something in the other man's eyes suddenly made John appear apprehensive. "No man takes what belongs to me!" he said loudly.

"I don't want anything you have. There's only one reason I'm here, and that's to find out who killed my parents and why," Ricardo said as he studied John.

A wary look suddenly flashed across John's face. "Robbers killed them."

"Possibly not," Victoria said quickly. "It seems that the witness to the ambush said assassins killed Robert and his family and made it look like robbers did it."

"I'm going to find the two men," Ricardo said in a cold voice.

John was angry now. "I don't care who you are or what you want. I want you gone!"

"I'll leave when I'm ready," Montoya said in a steady voice. "And not before."

The two men glared at each other momentarily. John suddenly whirled and walked out of the room. Ricardo glanced at his grandmother. She was sitting in a calm, unperturbed pose, smiling at him.

She had carefully analyzed the two men as they confronted one another. John was brash, domineering, and accustomed to men jumping at his command. Victoria noted that John was ill at ease in James's presence. He recognized that James was a powerful force, a man of strength and courage who did not flinch in the face of adversity. *He has no stomach for a face-to-face clash with James*, Victoria reasoned.

***

"Tends to be somewhat rude, doesn't he?" She said brightly.

"Doesn't anything bother you?" asked Montoya.

"I try not to let minor problems get in the way of what is important."

Ricardo perceived great depth in this woman. He walked over to her and sat down in a chair.

"I have the feeling you're always one step ahead of everyone. That we're sort of players on your stage," he said.

She smiled and gave him a kindly look. "I like intelligence and bravery and a thousand-and-one other attributes. You qualify in many of these areas," she said, and raised her eyebrows.

"Grandmother, I don't play other people's games."

"You think you're the master of your own destiny, and all that business. Well, you have a lot to learn," she said in a half-mocking voice.

Ricardo looked at her and laughed. "You're like a sunset that's always changing. I never know what you're thinking from minute to minute."

She gave him a broad smile and her eyes twinkled. "That's because I don't want you to."

"What is it that drives you so?" he asked.

She glanced at a picture of Charles Barringer over the fireplace. "His memory. What he built. I intend to see that the Barringer name and ranch carry on. John has no business sense, but he does follow my advice in business matters, and he holds this empire together. He may not be likable, but he gets the job done. William will carry on where he leaves off."

"William?" he said skeptically.

Victoria smiled. "What you see is a shell. I intend to fill that shell with all the necessary ingredients. He's a bright boy. All he needs is the right tutelage."

"What do you mean?"

"Tutelage means instruction or care. I'll see that he gets a lot of both."

"I'll bet you will," Ricardo said, smiling.

Victoria surveyed her grandson. "You have many of Charles's attributes: strength, intelligence, perseverance, courage. What I really want is for you to take over. You can't go back, so why not think about it?"

"Are you always plotting?"

Her blue eyes were piercing. "Above all else, the Barringer name and ranch must continue to prosper. This heritage will be passed on. Nothing must stand in our way."

"Where is John's wife?"

Victoria looked irritated. "I'm sorry to say that she left John and then divorced him. She lives in San Francisco."

"I'd like to ride around the grounds. Is that all right?" Ricardo asked.

"By all means. I'll have Pablo show you around. I suppose you would like to speak to someone in Spanish again."

"I haven't forgotten," he said, and grinned.

Thirty minutes later, Ricardo was being guided from one building to another by Pablo Enriquez, an older man with big buck teeth. When he smiled and his wide mouth opened, he looked like a ground squirrel. They spoke in Spanish.

"What brought you here, Pablo?"

"Many years ago I got in trouble with the Mexican police. I almost killed a man in a fight, and when I stopped running, I found myself here. The Barringers gave me the job of cook's helper and gardener. I've been here ever since. After a while, they even let me bring my wife and children up here."

"How are the Mexican people treated?"

"Mrs. Barringer treats us well. Her son is not a nice man and beats us now and then, but Mrs. Barringer makes him leave us alone most of the time."

They came out of the big barn where the prize breeding horse stock was kept. Enriquez wiped his brow with a handkerchief and pulled his pants up. They kept slipping down over his protruding stomach.

"Do you remember a man with a long L-shaped scar on his face?" Ricardo asked. "His name was Ed Graves."

A distasteful expression passed over Pablo's face. "Yes, I remember him. He was a bad one. He had a reputation with a gun before he came here. Scarface was hired to hunt down some *banditos* who were taking the Barringers' cattle. He did a good job and killed some of them. Then, when the patron died, John wanted to make him foreman, but Mrs. Barringer wouldn't allow it."

"Why not?"

"She didn't trust him. She and John had many loud arguments about it. But she finally won out, and Scarface left."

"Any idea where he might be now?"

"Yes," said Pablo. "He has a ranch near Fort Huachuca. At least, that's what I heard."

***

Victoria Barringer sat at the head of the large pecan dining table. Her regalia was, as always, flawless.

John Barringer sat at the opposite end of the long table. The guests on both sides included Mr. and Mrs. Ralph Bertram and Mr. and Mrs. Harry Palmer. Ricardo Montoya and William Barringer rounded out the dinner party of eight.

Montoya had changed from his Mexican clothing to tight buckskin pants with matching leather vest over a dark blue shirt. A bright gold bandanna hung loosely around his neck, and a tan Stetson had taken the place of his sombrero. He had also switched saddles and horses. Ricardo Montoya had become James Barringer.

Harry Palmer, the lawyer, discreetly watched James and John, noting their intense dislike for one another, which they were barely able to hold back. John refused to talk directly to James. William Barringer sat hunched near his grandmother, looking like he wished he was someplace…anyplace…else.

Much of the early dinner conversation had centered around Ricardo and his life in Mexico.

"What are your plans now?" Palmer asked James.

"I wanted to find out about my ancestry, and I've done that," said James. "There's one other thing I intend to do, and that's to find my parents' killers."

"How do you expect to do that? It was years and years ago, and there are no witnesses," said Palmer.

"This is hardly the conversation for a dinner party," said Victoria.

Ricardo glanced at his grandmother and then back at Palmer. "One of the men had a scar down his face and across his chin."

John Barringer choked on a piece of beef he was swallowing. He grabbed a glass of water and downed it. His dark eyes were mere slits as he looked at James.

Victoria sat frozen in her chair. Her lips were pressed tightly together as she carefully studied her son and James.

"What are you saying?" John growled.

"I think Scarface was a man who rode for this outfit for a while. His name was Ed Graves," James said in a steady voice. "Do you know where he is?"

John jumped to his feet. "You lie!"

"Both of you, sit down!" Victoria commanded. "I'll not have this kind of talk at my table. James, you're out of line to bring up such allegations and accusations. John, if you can't control your emotions, then you're not the man I think you are."

The matriarch was totally in command, and for a few moments there was absolute silence in the room. The two men slowly sat down again.

"Now then, that's better," said Victoria, and her beautiful white teeth flashed a smile.

LEE BISHOP

CHAPTER 8

Seven Apache warriors sat on their haunches around a small fire outside Sky Walker's wickiup on the San Carlos Indian Reservation. They talked of the old days when they had run free and raided into Mexico for cattle and women. Sky Walker was a Chiricahua chief, who had brought his people to the reservation the previous year. Many promises had been made about unlimited food, clothing, blankets, and housing. None of the promises had been kept.

Sky Walker was very tall for an Apache. At six-foot-four, he towered over most of his companions. He wore a long cotton shirt, loincloth, and supple Apache boots of soft leather, which could be pulled up over his knees as protection against cactus. His hair was long and bound by a red cloth wrapped around his head. An empty cartridge belt encircled his waist.

"We want you to lead us," said a short, stocky brave. "The families are ready."

Sky Walker stared into the fire. He hated the abysmal life they had been living. They had been herded together with hundreds of other Apaches, many of them from bands that were longtime antagonists. This created an uneasiness among all the groups.

The Office of Indian Affairs had attempted to force the Apaches to become farmers. In almost slave-labor fashion, the braves had been forced to hack out irrigation ditches. The men felt this was women's work and deeply resented the loss of face. They were unfamiliar with and disliked the white man's laws, court system, and police force made up of other Apaches. These reservation police were considered traitors for crossing over and working for the white man. The Apache women gathered hay for the soldiers and often sold themselves for a mirror or some trinket.

Food handed out weekly at the reservation agency was of poor quality and lasted only four or five days at most. The agents usually sold the best of the rations privately for their own profit.

But what Sky Walker found even worse was the boredom; the minutes, hours, and days filled with nothing. The men whiled away the hours gambling, singing, and telling stories of the old days when they could go wherever they chose and were proud of their capabilities.

Sky Walker looked around at the circle of men. "The white eyes come by the hundreds and thousands. For every one we kill, ten take his place. The yellow metal continues to draw them."

The braves stirred the sand with sticks. Red Arrow, the Apache who had spoken earlier, said, "Tell us what is in your heart."

"My heart is sad because we cannot stay here, and the white man will not let us live as we have for thousands of years. Yet, I see no happy ending. The blue coats are too many and armed too well."

Red Arrow was a much smaller man than Sky Walker. The sub-chief had a fierce look, accented by cold eyes, large cheekbones, a hawk like nose, and a broad mouth curving downward at the corners. He had a big chest, thick arms and legs, and was known for his prowess in hand-to-hand combat.

"It is better to die like a man than to live like a dog," said Red Arrow.

"You have been talking about taking more than two hundred braves, women, and children," said Sky Walker in his slow, steady manner. "Are you prepared for the women and children to die also?

"The Sierra Madres await us. When we get to Mexico, we can live as men ought to, raiding and stealing cattle and horses," said Red Arrow.

"Leaving here is not the problem," Sky Walker pointed out. "But we must get to the southern mountains before the army troops ride us down."

Several of the other Indians nodded their heads in agreement.

"To move such a large group calls for planning. I have a plan," said Sky Walker.

***

Two days later, Horace Demming, the San Carlos Indian agent, was overseeing the distribution of meat and flour to the Indians from the main supply building. The squaws were lined up for a block waiting to get their meager rations. Demming was a big man with a long, dark beard. His pants and shirt were dirty, and he looked as if he never bathed. A .44 caliber revolver was stuck in his waist band.

Six Indian police were scattered around the supply building, a long rectangular structure made entirely of mud bricks. The police had on blue army shirts and carried rifles.

One of the better-looking squaws walked up to Demming, smiled, and rubbed his stomach with her hand. He grinned and gave his full attention to her. At the same moment, Red Arrow slipped around the corner of the building and into the supply area. A supply worker inside screamed. Demming grabbed the handle of his revolver, but too late. The squaw buried the blade of a long knife in his stomach. His eyes bulged out and he fell to the ground with a groan.

As if a slow-motion panorama had suddenly been sped up, the line of squaws disintegrated into dozens of Indians running in various directions. Their targets were the Indian police, and they converged on their prey like hawks on pigeons. Their first target was the rifles, and the squaws held on regardless of how hard the Indian police tried to jerk the weapons free. Several of the police drew their knives and slashed at the women, but the braves arrived and quickly dispatched four of the police. The other two tried to run but were caught and quickly killed.

Supplies had been captured without a shot being fired. Horses and wagons were brought around and the loot was piled in.

Nearly half a mile away, two troopers stood and talked next to a corral that held thirty-five horses for the Indian police and a small detachment of soldiers. Fort Apache was twenty miles to the north. The soldiers continued talking even after they saw the three mounted Indian police approaching. The taller of the two troopers call out. "Is everything all right over there?"

Red Arrow answered by dropping the end of his rifle until it pointed directly at the soldier's chest. The man had a surprised look on his face when Red Arrow pulled the trigger. The other Indians shot the second man.

It took less than a minute for the braves to herd the horses out of the corral and head back to the supply building. Most of the braves who mounted the horses preferred to ride bareback.

A crowd of several hundred Indians had gathered to watch. It was the largest breakout that had ever occurred on the reservation. About forty braves accompanied the supply wagons filled with provisions, heading southeast with the women and children. Their intent was to reach the Dragoon Mountains and the temporary protection of the rocky gorges, ravines, and sheer cliffs.

The main band of Apache warriors went in a southwesterly direction toward the mining settlements of Kearney, Hayden, and Winkelman. Sky Walker's plan was to draw the primary force of cavalry away from the women and children and make them follow the mounted braves as they burned, pillaged, raped, and murdered.

The war party included two braves for each horse. Acting as partners, one brave would hold onto the horse's tail and run along behind the animal while the other Indian rode. They switched positions every few miles. Apache warriors could cover fifty miles per day on foot. By using the change-off method, they were able to cover a distance equal to what the best cavalry could ride.

It took nearly half a day for the troopers at the supply area to reach Fort Apache and warn them of the breakout. The lieutenant in charge of the food disbursement and the horses was broken in rank on the spot. Slightly more than two hundred cavalry soldiers were assembled and ready to depart at daybreak the following morning.

But Sky Walker's group of warriors was nearing the mining camps by mid-afternoon. Their first victims on the rampage were a column of ore wagons heading toward Winkelman. The Apaches waited, hidden on a boulder-strewn hill, until the six wagons and their accompanying guards were even with them. The Indians opened fire, killing several of the miners and the horses pulling the first wagon. Then they swarmed like ants over the miners and their wagons. Several of the white men were tied to wagon wheels and slowly tortured to death. A young rancher and his wife were killed quickly when their buggy rounded the bend in the road and bumped into the front ranks of the Indians.

Before nightfall, a surveying patrol and two hunters had also fallen victim to the war party.

Counting the twelve dead on the reservation, the raiding had killed thirty-two men and women in twenty-four hours. At dusk they ate dried beef and corn and fell asleep immediately. Before three o'clock, the guards silently passed among the sleeping figures and quietly woke them.

The shadowy figures blended in with the rocks as they silently converged on the four corrals where the Winkelman miners kept the largest number of their horses and mules. The two guards were quickly knifed, and the Indians made their way among the horses, picking out the best stock.

It wasn't until the seventy braves were mounted and riding through the tent camp that the miners came to life. The Apaches made one pass through the tent city, setting fire to many of the tents and shooting the half-awake miners as they came out.

Red Arrow galloped in circles and used a tomahawk to hack down five miners as he leaned from the saddle. The camp was alive now with screaming men, gunshots, and galloping horses, and the flickering firelight from the burning tents cast eerie moving shadows over the battle.

As fast as it had begun, it was over. Sky Walker pulled his braves out of the fight as soon as the miners began to rally a stronger defense. Eighteen miners were dead and twenty-three wounded. The Apache band had lost five men, and three were wounded. They stopped and regrouped a mile from the site of the battle.

"Let us destroy the next mining camp!" Red Arrow shouted.

The braves whooped, yelled, and shot off their guns in the air. The heady feeling of victory, of vanquishing one's enemies, was upon them. They were men again, not animals to be treated with contempt. Sky Walker watched the scene unfold around him and let his men have their moment of glory. Five minutes later, the rear guard joined the main band. The miners' horses and mules had been scattered after the Apaches had taken their first pick. The white men were not thinking of pursuit.

"Hear me!" Sky Walker said loudly. "This has been a day to rejoice!"

The Apaches' war cries echoed off the surrounding rock walls.

"But we must have the wisdom of our fathers. We have brought much glory to ourselves, but five braves are dead. Who will fill the positions next to you where those Apaches rode?"

The Indians were silent and listened intently to their leader.

"For every man we lose, there is no one to take his place. After ten more battles, we will have no warriors left."

Sky Walker stopped and let his words strike home.

"So we must not go against large numbers of white eyes. We must hit and run, kill and steal, and work our way south without losing more braves. There is no honor in dying, only in raiding!" Sky Walker shouted, and raised his war lance.

The braves responded with the loudest demonstration yet. The chief urged his horse forward, and the large group of warriors and stolen horses stretched out behind.

Five units of cavalry converged on the small mining settlements after the telegraph had flashed word of the major assault. But the Apache band had already made its way through the Tortilla Mountains without being sighted, and was outside Oracle Junction by the following evening. Four traders and their two supply wagons were the next victims. The Indians jumped from a ravine and were upon the wagons in a wave of brown bodies. Sky Walker was elated over the contents of the wagons, which included food, medicine, clothing, boots, arms, and ammunition. He ordered the braves to load the spoils on the extra horses, and they moved on.

The band entered the foothills of the Santa Catalina Mountains, northeast of Tucson, as night fell. There the Apaches rested, but by daybreak of the third day they were heading southeast into the Rincon Range. They stayed out of sight to elude the pursuing cavalry units. By nightfall they had reached their rendezvous point in the low-lying Whetstone Mountains. Sky Walker had chosen the area because he could see for miles across the high plains.

Meanwhile, the main party of Apaches, including the women and children, had safely reached the Dragoon Mountains. They traveled only at night and were under strict orders from Sky Walker not to let themselves be seen. A sub-chief, Sitting Bear, was in charge of the slow-moving band. For the next two nights, they moved westward toward the meeting point. As they passed across a range near St. David, the younger bucks applied pressure to Sitting Bear, asking that they be allowed to attack a lone ranch house atop a small hill.

Sitting Bear agreed, and twenty of the braves detached themselves from the group and made their way across the grasslands toward the adobe ranch house owned by Cal Gentry.

The Apaches' first mistake was a disastrous one. Cal Gentry had been the target of more than one marauding band of Indians and bandits over the past ten years. His house was a simple fortress-like structure, built in the form of a long rectangle. The walls of the house were nearly two feet thick and penetrated only by gun portals and one door. The huge oak door was hung on heavy iron hinges and locked from the inside by two sliding logs. The walls extended three feet above the roof, so defenders could climb up to the top of the building and fire down at attackers.

Cal, his wife, Margarita, and their two boys lived in the house. Four ranch hands stayed in a nearby bunk house. Cal raised cattle, but he was best known for his hams, which were prized throughout the southern Arizona Territory.

Gentry was taciturn and stubborn. He refused to leave his lands even though Apaches killed his stock, stole his horses, and attacked his men. Seven had been wounded or killed. The Apaches were not interested in his pigs, and it was this venture that brought Cal the most revenue.

Sitting Bear's braves had been spotted when they were still a quarter mile from the ranch house. Gentry, his two teenage boys, and the four cowhands were all armed with repeating rifles and revolvers. Margarita Gentry carried a sawed-off, double-barreled shotgun and strapped a belt of shells around her waist.

"Can't have been here before," Gentry said to one of the hands. "There's only about twenty of 'em."

Cal was on top of the house with the four cowboys. His wife and sons were down inside waiting for his commands.

Most of the Apaches crouched down in the grass to the west of the house, or were gathered near the sides of the bunk house. Two braves worked their way through the grass and ran at the front door.

"Now!" Gentry yelled.

Both braves reached the front door but went down in a blaze of fire. One of them was shot through the back as he attempted to crawl to safety. The Apaches released a shower of arrows, and two bucks with rifles fired at the gun portals. Their shots went wild.

Cal and his men fired at the Indians crouched in the grass. Three braves were hit. Then the cowboys ducked down and ran around until they were opposite the bunk house. Again they fired as a group, and another Apache went down. Inside the home, Race Gentry, the eldest son, was looking out the loophole on the south side of the house. He took careful aim and fired. A tall brave, who had been running toward the fortress, took the bullet in his stomach and pitched forward on his face. Race aimed a second time and killed him.

The Apaches had had enough. They grabbed two wounded braves and dragged them back out of range. Cal picked up his old buffalo gun, which was made for distance shooting. He sighted carefully down the barrel of the long rifle and pulled the trigger. The slug hit the last retreating Indian a split second before the sound of the gunshot reached the Apaches.

Sitting Bear's war party had been decimated. Five bucks were dead and another three wounded. They had killed or wounded none of the enemy and had left even before they could steal a horse from the corral.

On the roof, the cowboys were rejoicing. Five Indians were dead, and the Mexican government in Sonora paid one hundred pesos for each scalp. Cal would allow his ranch hands to split the money between them.

The main band continued eastward that night until they hooked up with Sky Walker and his group in the Whetstone Mountains. The chief took the news without showing emotion, but he was disappointed that Sitting Bear had shown weakness and that so many braves had died needlessly.

The band now moved south, planning to skirt Fort Huachuca, which had the biggest concentration of army troops in the Arizona Territory. Sky Walker had guessed, and rightly so, that the soldiers would never expect his band to take such a dangerous route.

LEE BISHOP

CHAPTER 9

John Barringer lashed his horse with a quirt, and the big animal put its last ounces of energy into the long run down the hill to the small ranch house on the plains north of Fort Huachuca. He dismounted, tied his horse to the hitching rail in front of the main building, and quickly walked up the porch steps.

Leaning against a veranda post smoking a cigar was the owner of the house, Ed Graves. He was a man of medium height and build, with graying sandy hair. A long scar ran down his left cheek and across his chin. His light blue eyes had very little color, which gave them a strange, translucent appearance. The scar and his strange eyes left an indelible impression on all who met him. Graves was a very calm man.

"What brings you here?" he asked Barringer.

Barringer was in an agitated state. "We got troubles. That kid we couldn't find when we killed my brother? Well, he turned up. Seems that some Mex saw us do the killin' and then found the kid and raised him in Mexico."

Graves nodded his head in understanding, but as usual Barringer couldn't tell if Scarface was looking at him or through him. "You've got a problem all right."

Barringer's dark eyes flashed. "It's a problem we both have. The Mexican identified your scar, and by asking around, this troublemaker learned your name."

"What's his name?"

"Ricardo Montoya. Seems he cast a big shadow in Mexico. Was the foreman of a big ranch. He ain't the type that scares," said Barringer.

"You think he'll be coming to pay me a visit?"

"Yup, and soon," said Barringer. "How many men you got ridin' for you now?"

A small smile appeared on Graves' face. "You still measuring men by how much fire power they've got behind 'em?"

Barringer's large, swarthy face showed his anger, but he knew better than to bring on a confrontation with Graves.

"You won't be thinking it's funny when he shows up. He looks just like my father. I swear, the resemblance is uncanny."

Graves said nothing as he looked out over his property. "If you want me to kill him, it'll cost you."

Barringer's dark eyes narrowed and his face turned red. "You don't think I'd hold still for that...."

Graves shifted his eyes and stared at Barringer. John suddenly felt an uneasiness and stopped talking. He remembered that Ed Graves could kill without showing the slightest hint of emotion.

"What I mean is that I paid you for the job years ago. And, I put up the collateral so you could get the ranch," Barringer said.

"This is a different time and a different place, John. For killing Montoya, it'll cost you five thousand dollars."

"Five thousand!" said Barringer in disbelief.

"I need some of that new shorthorn breeding stock, and that should about cover it," said Graves.

Barringer swallowed hard and choked back his emotions. "Agreed! Let me know when it's done, and you can pick up the money from the Patagonia bank."

John turned and started down the steps.

"By the way," said Graves, "give my best to your mother."

Barringer glanced over his shoulder but said nothing. He didn't appreciate the humor.

***

As John Barringer rode away from the ranch, Ricardo Montoya watched him go from a small stand of trees atop a hill overlooking Graves' ranch. *Smart place to build*, thought Ricardo. It was too close to the fort for any marauding Apaches to attack. They wouldn't want the cavalry on their trail that quickly. And he had a ready market for his beef, too.

Ricardo mounted his horse and went back the way he had come until he was two miles away from Graves's ranch. He rested the horse, ate a cold meal, and waited until sundown. When it was dark, he rode to within a quarter mile of the ranch headquarters, picketed the horse, and walked slowly up to the buildings. The barn and cook shack were dark, but lights were still visible in the main house and bunk house. Montoya made a half circle around the smaller buildings and came up to the rear of the ranch house. There was no noise from within, but the main room was well lighted with lanterns.

Montoya went around to the front the house and peered into one of the small windows. He saw Scarface behind a desk, writing in his daily record book. Ricardo drew his revolver, opened the front door, and walked in.

"I've been expecting you, Montoya. You do look like Charles Barringer. The resemblance is remarkable."

"I want to know who was with you when you ambushed my family," said Ricardo.

A cowboy suddenly appeared in the doorway that led to the kitchen, to the right and slightly behind Montoya.

"Freeze!" the cowboy ordered. "Now drop the gun."

Ricardo did as he was ordered.

Graves got up from behind his desk, walked around it, and stood before Ricardo. "I wanted to see what you looked like before I killed you," he said.

The cowboy advanced into the room, still aiming his revolver at Montoya. Ricardo looked at the cowboy and then back at Graves. Montoya suddenly grabbed Scarface by the shoulders and yanked his body around to create a shield between himself and the man with the gun. Using his full power, Ricardo jammed Graves up against his cowhand. With tremendous force, Montoya shoved the pair backward until the cowboy fell over a small table. Ricardo threw Scarface on top of the cowboy, pulled his knife from its sheath, and placed it against the struggling rancher's throat. Graves' eyes bulged out and he grunted.

"Tell your man to drop his gun and quit struggling or I'll cut your throat from ear to ear!" said Ricardo.

"Do what he says, Bill."

The cowboy released his grip on the gun and let it fall to the floor. Ricardo grabbed Graves by the vest and hauled him to an upright position.

"You," Montoya said to the cowboy. "Get out of here. Tell the rest of the cowhands that your boss and I are going for a ride. If anyone makes a play, he dies first."

The thin cowboy got slowly to his feet and backed out the door. Ricardo retrieved his revolver after he had taken

Graves's gun from his holster. Montoya heard the cowboys running up to the house. He grabbed Scarface by the front of his shirt and pushed him over to the front door.

"Tell them we're riding out. Make it good."

Graves glanced at Montoya, then at the door. "We're coming out. Nobody does anything unless I give the order!" Scarface yelled.

Ricardo had one hand on the back of Graves's shirt collar and the other holding a revolver to his back. They walked past the group of cowhands and mounted two of the horses.

"One of you ride over to the Barringer ranch and tell John Barringer that I have Graves. I'll be waiting for him at the base of the mountain range just north of here," said Ricardo.

As the two men rode away, they heard a cowboy saying, "I wonder if Barringer will help him."

A rider was dispatched to the Barringer ranch within minutes.

Two hours passed before Ricardo and his captive reached the foothills of the low mountain range. He tied Scarface and covered him with a blanket. Montoya sat back against a boulder, smoked a cigarette, and looked at the stars. He began thinking of Maria Bustamante, her warmth, the touch of her body, and the sweet smell of her hair. *Peace*, he thought. *Someday I'll find peace*.

At sunrise he awoke. Graves was twisting and turning, trying to get comfortable in a different position. Ricardo got up, started a small fire, and cooked coffee and breakfast. He untied Graves's legs and tied his hands in front of him, rather than behind, so he could eat. They had spoken scarcely a dozen words since Ricardo had captured him.

Montoya looked up to see Graves studying him. Scarface's light blue eyes amazed Ricardo. He reminded Ricardo of El Lobo.

"What do you want?" Graves asked.

Montoya sipped his coffee and looked out across the grasslands. "I want to know who was with you when you shot my family."

"Suppose I tell ya. What happens to me?"

Ricardo fixed his charcoal eyes on Graves. "You'll get a fair chance to defend yourself."

Graves studied the big man for a moment and then looked away, apparently wanting more than a fair chance.

The morning and afternoon passed before Barringer and his riders appeared on the horizon. Montoya put some green grass on the fire to create smoke and make his position known. Ricardo had chosen the spot carefully so that he could command an entire one-hundred-and-eighty degree view in front and slightly behind him. He had the horses tethered higher up the hill behind a massive pile of rocks. In an emergency, he could reach the horses and continue to climb into the mountain range without becoming an easy target. One man could hold off a dozen attackers in this rocky mountain terrain.

Montoya counted eight riders with Barringer as they drew closer. Ricardo looked below him at the group and did not recognize any of the regular cowboys from the ranch. John had obviously hand-picked the men to accompany him, and Montoya could guess what type of men Barringer had brought with him...men who would do anything for money.

"Montoya, you've got a friend of mine. Let him go!" Barringer yelled.

"This is one of the men who killed your brother," Ricardo answered.

"You've got no proof of that," said John.

Montoya pushed Graves out from behind the rocks. Scarface stood there in the line of fire, looking alarmed by the turn of events.

"You want to tell me now?" Ricardo asked quietly.

"What the hell are you doing?" Graves said in an angry voice.

Barringer looked up at the two men talking to one another and seemed to come to a decision. He raised his rifle and fired. Montoya was expecting the move and stepped backward behind the boulder, but Barringer wasn't aiming at Ricardo. The bullet slammed into Graves's chest and knocked him over backward. His blue eyes were wide as he looked up at Montoya.

Ricardo knelt down beside him. "Who was the second man?"

Scarface opened his mouth, coughed, and exhaled slowly.

Seeing that he was dead, Montoya ran in a crouched position to where the horses were tied. He mounted his animal and led the second horse as he climber higher into the mountain range. Barringer and his men fired a few shots after Ricardo, but they could not see enough of him to get a clear shot.

Using an animal path, Montoya rode among the large boulders and rock outcroppings, staying at a medium elevation as he traversed the mountain range in a half circle. He was looking for a vantage point from which to send a few shots at his pursuers and discourage them from following. The route was difficult. Ricardo walked the horses through a narrow ravine, which ended up looking westward from the mountain range.

At a point overlooking the grasslands below, he pulled his horse to a halt. He couldn't believe the sight below him.

An Apache band of nearly two hundred men, women, and children was stretched out for a quarter of a mile as they headed south toward Mexico. Ricardo quickly counted about ninety braves, and realized that this was one of the largest mass escapes to take place in the past five years.

He moved laterally with the horses for another two hundred yards so that John Barringer and his men would come to the same vantage point. He dismounted and pulled a Winchester .44 with an extra-long barrel from its scabbard. The weapon had an extra rear sight, which could be raised for greater accuracy at long distances.

Seeing that Barringer and his men were now looking at the Apaches, Montoya rested his arms on the boulder in front of him and set the sights for three hundred yards. He placed the polished wood stock against his cheek and squeezed off the first shot. The rifle bucked against his shoulder, and he watched a brave topple off his horse.

Barringer and his men heard the shot and saw the Indian fall.

"That crazy fool!" one of the cowboys yelled. The Barringer hands dismounted and situated themselves behind rocks and boulders.

The chief motioned and twenty of his braves headed toward the foothills with their horses at a dead run. A particularly fierce warrior was at the front of the first wave of horsemen. Montoya was ready. In rapid succession, he fired six shots from the rifle. Four of them found their marks, hitting either Apaches or their horses. The warrior's horse was struck and went down in a cloud of dust. The Apache sub-chief hit the ground with such force that it nearly knocked him unconscious.

Now a round of gunfire from the nine Barringer riders found its mark, and three more Indians were hit before the wave of Apaches reached the protection of the boulders and rocks at the bottom of the foothills. The Indians tried to advance but were driven back by blistering fire from the cowhands.

***

The Apache chief watched for a few moments more and then gave the signal for retreat. Two braves remained and kept up a steady fire while the others gathered their wounded and headed back to the main band. Sky Walker pulled the column westward out of gunshot range and halted his band.

Red Arrow urged an all-out attack. "They number only ten or twelve men in all," he said.

Sky Walker remained impassive. "They are well armed and shoot well. We would lose a great many braves before we killed them. This we will not do."

Red Arrow was furious. "We will lose face today if we do not avenge our dead!"

"When we reach the mountains in Mexico, you will be able to avenge many wrongs. But no more of our men will die today," Sky Walker said with finality.

The Apache chief ordered two dozen braves to remain in the area for another day to keep the cowboys from reaching Fort Huachuca and warning the soldiers.

***

Once he realized the fight was over, Ricardo continued climbing into the mountains. He headed north for another two hours, then worked his way down. He rode westward for five miles and then turned south and worked his way along the eastern edge of the Santa Rita Mountains. He rode all night, and by daybreak the next morning he had reached the Barringer Ranch.

He paced the floor in the living room while he waited for his grandmother to be awakened and notified of his return.

***

Victoria Barringer finally appeared, looking as regal as ever. "James, is anything really so important that I must be awakened at this uncivilized hour?" she asked.

He quickly told her of the Apache movement in the direction of the Barringer Ranch.

"What a time for John to be gone. I don't know where he's off to," she said.

Ricardo could see her sharp mind turning over as she mapped and analyzed various strategies.

"Your son won't be back for another day," Ricardo said. "An Apache war party is between his ranch hands and Fort Huachuca."

Her penetrating blue eyes bore into Ricardo.

"I paid a visit to Ed Graves. He never denied that he was in on the ambush," said Ricardo.

His grandmother was gazing at him intently but said nothing.

"John and his men showed up. He killed Graves before I could find out who the second man was. He would have killed me if he'd had the chance," Ricardo said in a calm voice.

Victoria's mind was churning. Was John involved in the murder of his brother and his brother's family? Was he that jealous of his brother that he would have him assassinated? Did his mind snap? *Or, perhaps he wasn't involved at all*, she thought. *Only time will tell. It's been so long ago, it's like revisiting history.*

Grandmother and grandson looked intently at one another. But, Victoria suddenly jerked her attention back to the present problem of the Apaches.

"I'll have a talk with John when he returns. Now, what is your thought about the Indians?"

Ricardo walked to the front window and turned to address his grandmother. "We had a lot of experience with the Apaches on Don Diego Salazar's hacienda. From my experience, one thing was always sure...you never want to fight a large group of Indians unless you have to. They must be watched and know that they are being watched."

Victoria shook her head and appeared impatient. "Forgive me, James, but I don't follow your line of reasoning."

"What I suggest is that I take a group of cowboys and intercept the Apaches and escort them southward across the ranch. This is to make sure that small groups don't break loose to steal and kill," said Ricardo.

"You mean watch them from afar and let them know they are being watched. Is that it?"

"Yes."

"What about the cavalry?" she asked.

"I already sent a rider to the fort. However, my experience with the Mexican rurales has been that they do not move swiftly to solve a problem. And, I would guess that the Apaches will be in Mexico before the U. S. cavalry reaches them," Montoya speculated.

Victoria smiled. "I place high regard on intelligence, James," she said with a twinkle in her eye.

***

Within an hour, Montoya had collected every cowboy in the vicinity of the main ranch. More than forty riders waited outside the house for Ricardo and his grandmother to appear. Ricardo came down the main stairs toward his grandmother, who waited near the front door. He was dressed in Mexican clothing and could see the questioning look in her eyes.

"I have many relatives and friends on the ranchos at the head of the Sierra Madres. Those people will need my help, because this is where the Indians will go," Ricardo explained.

As always, it was difficult for Ricardo to discern what his grandmother was thinking as she studied him. "You will be back," she said. It was more of a statement than a question.

"Yes, I'll be back. I intend to find out who that second man was," Ricardo said in a level voice.

"What is meant to be shall be," said Victoria. She turned and moved through the doorway onto the veranda. Her movements were fluid and graceful, and her dignity and bearing were flawless. Every eye was upon her. "I have every confidence in the ability of the men who ride for the Barringer Ranch. My grandson James will lead you. We have talked over what course of action to follow, and he and I agree," she said in a clear voice.

Her eyes were slightly hooded as she scanned the audience. Ricardo smiled at his grandmother and then swung into the saddle. He touched the palomino with his knees and the big horse jumped forward.

The horsemen rode for three hours before they caught the trail of the Apache band. In another hour they had overtaken the steadily moving procession. Ricardo spread his men out in single file, and they rode parallel to the Indians.

***

Sky Walker spotted the riders first and conferred with his sub-chiefs. As usual, Red Arrow urged that an all-out attack be mounted.

"It is humiliating to let them watch us and do nothing," the hawk-nosed sub-chief maintained.

"We will make no more widows this day," said Sky Walker. "We must reach the Mexican mountains before the horse soldiers overtake us. Our band must remain strong and unified if we are to survive. We have lost too many warriors foolishly."

"It is in our blood to fight!" snarled Red Arrow.

"Victories go to the wise," Sky Walker said firmly.

Red Arrow wheeled his horse and raced to the head of the column.

Near nightfall, the Apaches reached the border. Sky Walker called a brief halt while the band ate and rested. It was his plan to march all night to reach the Sierra Madres and safety in the rocky crags.

Sky Walker rode toward the cowboys for several hundred yards. He sat on his horse and watched Ricardo giving instructions to the cowhands. The sight of the tall man on the gold horse was clearly etched in his mind.

CHAPTER 10

Ricardo Montoya and his brother, Rafael, threw their arms around each other and pounded one another on the back. Ricardo had sent word for his brother to meet him at a location over a mile from El Rancho Grande. The two brothers acted like children as they pounded each other on the shoulders and pummeled one another playfully. They looked much alike with their dark hair and eyes, although Ricardo was the tallest by several inches.

"It's good to be back," said Ricardo. "I've missed you. I've missed everyone."

"The hacienda is not the same without you, Brother," said Rafael.

"Listen, Rafael. The reason I have come back is that a large band of Apaches has jumped the reservation at San Carlos in the Arizona Territory. They number about two hundred."

Rafael looked surprised. "Two hundred!"

"Only half of them are warriors. The rest are women and children," said Ricardo. "They are going to use the mountains as a base to raid and burn from. All the ranchers must be warned."

Rafael nodded his head in understanding.

Ricardo continued. "As in the old days, the Salazar and Bustamante ranchos are the ones in gravest danger. You will have to organize scouting teams and pull back the scattered families and vaqueros from the far reaches of the hacienda."

"I understand," said Rafael.

"Who does Salazar have commanding the ranch operations?"

"His son," said Rafael.

"You mean Francisco?"

"Don't laugh," said Rafael. "The young man has done well. He tries hard, even though his father screams at him a lot. He comes to me privately and asks for advice every day."

There was a look of doubt in Ricardo's eyes.

"Listen, Brother," said Rafael. "When you ran things, you did everything yourself. You didn't leave much room for Francisco or anyone else. You charge like a bull."

Ricardo laughed. "What you say is true. No man is perfect. How goes it with you?"

Rafael shrugged his shoulders. "I can't understand it, but Don Diego seems to rely on me more and more. I thought he might have trained someone else to be head of his bodyguard, but he hasn't."

"He knows he can't do without a Montoya," said Ricardo.

The two men laughed. Ricardo and Rafael talked for a while about the ranch operations, friends, and what strategy to use against the Apaches.

"I've got some good news that I was saving," said Rafael. "I'm going to marry Lupe Zapata, the daughter of Eduardo Zapata, the mayor of Santa Ana."

Ricardo slapped his brother on the back. "Is she the one with the narrow waist and the long legs?"

"Yes, yes," Rafael said proudly.

"Is she the one with the full body and the beautiful lips?"

"Yes. That's her," Rafael said, and beamed. Then suddenly the smile faded from his face. "How do you know so much about her?"

"Good news gets around," Ricardo replied.

"What do you mean?" Rafael said suspiciously.

Ricardo laughed. "I used to call on the girl, Catrina Vasquez, who lived next door to Lupe in Santa Ana."

Rafael's angry look dissolved into a grin. "You did that to me on purpose."

Ricardo threw his arms around his brother's neck. "I'm really glad to hear the news."

"Tell me about yourself now, for I have heard very little," said Rafael.

Ricardo explained about the Barringers and the killing of Ed Graves.

"Do you really think you are this James Barringer?"

Ricardo nodded. "From the photographs I have seen, yes. Charles Barringer, the founder of the ranch, was my grandfather. I look very much like him."

Rafael frowned. "That doesn't mean much. Remember, you and I look alike. In fact, we are alike."

"We are brothers. We always will be," said Ricardo.

"What will you do now?" asked Rafael.

Ricardo looked in the direction of the Bustamante ranch. "Don Carlos will need help. He doesn't have nearly enough men to protect himself from raids."

"I don't suppose seeing Maria Bustamante again is any incentive?" said Rafael.

Ricardo gave his brother a sly smile. "Maybe a little bit."

The brothers drank coffee and ate lunch at the campsite. Ricardo checked over his horse's cinch strap as Rafael stroked the big palomino on the nose.

Ricardo glanced at his brother. "Tell me what happened when El Lobo's possessions arrived back here."

"Don Diego was furious. He screamed and carried on for two days. He also had me call in extra men. I think he was afraid that Don Carlos might come for him," said Rafael. "Also, a letter came from the state government. It may have been a warning."

"If Don Carlos sent messages to other ranchers, as he said he would, I would guess that Don Diego has lost face," said Ricardo.

Rafael nodded in agreement. "He has not been to any social functions since then."

Ricardo had finished checking his saddle gear. He mounted the palomino and looked intently at his brother. "Be careful, Rafael. Don Diego has a twisted mind. He might even attempt to get back at me through you."

"I'll be careful, but I don't see that problem arising. He needs me," Rafael said, and grinned.

The brothers said their farewells, and Ricardo rode away. Rafael stood and watched his brother until he was just a speck in the distance.

Ricardo made good time as he headed for the southern line camps that Bustamante had established at the base of the Sierra Madres. Two vaqueros were at one camp and three at the other. Ricardo had them scatter the cattle so that the Apaches would not have an entire herd to move into the mountains. He told the vaqueros to report back to the main ranch and warn Don Carlos. Then, he headed north along a route he guessed would intersect with the Indians' southward route. He rested atop a hill with a sweeping view of the surrounding countryside.

By midafternoon he spotted the Apache scouts who were well in advance of the main party. The band of Indians passed a half mile to the west of his position as they entered the foothills of the mountains. Ricardo mounted Oro and moved the animal to a spot where he was in plain view of the Apaches.

***

Sky Walker saw Ricardo and recognized the tall man on the golden horse even before his scouts reached the chief to ask his advice.

"Do nothing," said Sky Walker.

"Let us ride him down," said one of the braves.

"Could your pony overtake the golden horse? Does he have men waiting in ambush? Why is he there in plain sight?" Sky Walker asked the young braves. "You must think. You must reason if you are to stay alive."

"It is an insult to let him watch us," one of the braves protested.

"It is only an insult if it bothers you. Small things do not bother warriors. Warriors block from their minds things that are unimportant. Our objective is the mountains and a safe camp for our women and children. Keep this uppermost in your minds," Sky Walker instructed his braves.

The scouts rode back to their positions and ignored Ricardo. Sky Walker never looked at him, but the tall man was on his mind. Sky Walker guessed he was a Mexican who had led cowboys north of the border and returned to Mexico to scout the Apache band. He would be one to remember and look out for.

***

Once the band entered the foothills, Ricardo backtracked until it was nearly dark. As night closed in, he could see the fires from the cavalry column that had stopped for the evening. Under an agreement signed by the presidents of both countries, American troops were allowed into Mexico to help the federal rurales capture the marauders.

The sentry stopped Ricardo a hundred yards from the camp. Montoya identified himself and was directed to the commanding officer's tent. He was announced, but a full five minutes went by before the tent flap parted and a young man's head and shoulders were visible.

"Come in," he said. "I am Lieutenant Kenneth Fredericks." He held the tent flap open while Montoya bent over and entered. A balding man of about fifty sat behind a folding table covered with maps. His face was sun burned and his eyes were unfriendly.

"State your business," said Captain Thomas Beeshore in a gruff manner.

Ricardo looked from Beeshore to the young blond Lieutenant Fredericks, who averted his eyes. Ricardo could sense that Beeshore did not like Mexicans.

"My name is Ricardo Montoya. I came to talk to you about the Indian band you are following."

"What about 'em?" said Beeshore.

"I have some idea of where they're going and what they plan to do," said Montoya.

"I doubt that," said Beeshore belligerently.

Montoya's eyes narrowed. "Then there's nothing for us to discuss," he said, and turned to leave.

"Wait a minute!" Beeshore said in a loud voice. "If you have something to say, say it."

Ricardo looked at the lieutenant. *He can't be over twenty-one*, Montoya thought, *and he's second in command to this fool.*

"The band is headed for the Sierra Madre Mountains due south of here. Some of the areas in the mountains are impenetrable. Half their number of braves could hold off twice or three times your number of men. We've fought the

Apaches for generations here, and after a while you get to know how they think. Should I go on?" Montoya said in an even, hard voice.

"Go on," said Beeshore.

"You have about one hundred and twenty-five men. You have the Apaches outnumbered, but when you go into the mountains, they'll be looking to ambush you. It's the only time you'll see them," said Montoya.

Beeshore's eyes were cold as they appraised Ricardo. "What's your point?"

"There have been tactics used that proved successful—"

The cavalry captain cut him off. "You're going to teach us tactics?" he said in a disgusted voice.

"I can see that your mind is not open to suggestions or new ideas," Montoya said in an even voice. "I have nothing further to talk to you about." Ricardo swung around and headed for the tent opening.

"I haven't dismissed you yet," said Beeshore.

Montoya stopped and turned.

"What do you mean?"

"I mean I haven't said you could go."

Montoya's eyes were blazing. "I come when I want, and I go when I want. You would do well to listen in the future. It might keep your men alive."

Ricardo slashed the tent flap open with his arm and angrily stomped out. He watered his horse and was preparing to leave when Lieutenant Fredericks approached him.

"Mr. Montoya, could you give us a moment of your time before you leave?" the young lieutenant asked.

"Yes."

"I'd like you to meet Top Sergeant Sam Kincaid. He's been fighting Apaches out here as long as you have," Fredericks said, and grinned.

Montoya and Kincaid nodded at each other. Fredericks looked around to make sure no one could hear them talk. "I'd like to apologize for the captain. He's just been transferred out here, too, and he's not happy about it," said Fredericks in a good-natured manner.

Ricardo gazed at the young man and then looked at Kincaid, a barrel-chested trooper with a weather-beaten face. Kincaid had a plug of chewing tobacco in his right cheek.

"You mean neither you nor Beeshore have had experience fighting Apaches?"

Fredericks looked chagrined. Kincaid was noncommittal, and his expression was stoical.

"That's right, but I'm sure we'll learn," said Fredericks with a nervous grin.

"You'll learn, all right," said Ricardo.

He suddenly felt sorry for the young trooper. Fredericks was asking for help in the only way he knew. Montoya walked over to him. "The Apaches will lead you where they want you to go. You won't get close to them in the mountains unless they want you to. If they let you get near, it will be to spring an ambush," Ricardo said in a steady voice.

"I understand," said Fredericks. "But what about our Apache scouts? They're supposed to guard against this happening to us."

"Apaches are Apaches. The scouts you use today were the ones who broke out of the reservation last time to rob and burn."

"How can that be?" Fredericks said.

"The scouts you're using are from a different band, probably Mimbres. The Apaches you are chasing are

Chiricahuas. Many Apache bands are natural enemies, so they sell themselves as scouts. It's expected," said Ricardo.

Fredericks looked at Sergeant Kincaid for assurance. The sergeant nodded his head in agreement with Montoya.

"But then aren't they trustworthy?" said Fredericks.

"Sometimes yes, sometimes no," said Ricardo. "I'd use a lot of troopers as advance scouts in addition to the Apaches. That way you have your own eyes out there."

"Can't tell the captain nothin'," said Kincaid. "He done learned it all in them Civil War stand-up battles. He don't think much of the 'paches."

"He doesn't think much of anyone," said Ricardo.

"That's the plain truth," said Kincaid.

"Gentlemen. Can we get back to the subject at hand?" said Fredericks.

Montoya smiled at the young man. "What else do you want to know?"

"As a form of strategy, what would you do?"

"I'd break the troops into large scouting parties," said Ricardo. "Have them cover the foothills every day looking for signs of raiding parties coming out into the flat country. The Apaches have to have supplies. They have to raid or go back to the reservation and be fed."

Fredericks nodded his head in understanding.

"How many of your troops are veterans?" Ricardo asked Kincaid.

"Not many," said the top sergeant. "Most have never seen combat."

Ricardo said nothing as he mounted his horse.

"Where will you be going?" Fredericks asked.

"The Apaches will raid the ranches and farms. Those people will need help," said Ricardo. "A last word of advice. If you get ambushed, get as many of your people together as you can and keep them in a group. Then retreat when it's dark. If you split your men into small groups, the Apaches will run you down."

The lieutenant looked somewhat angry and resentful. "We're the United States Army, and we've never lost a war!"

"You didn't win any battles with that type of a commander," Ricardo said, pointing at Captain Beeshore's tent.

Montoya let his words sink in and then touched his heels to Oro. The big stallion jumped forward and pounded away from the camp.

It was a long night's ride to the Bustamante ranch, and Ricardo maintained a slow, steady pace. The moon was bright, and he stayed in the open, flat country. Twice he came upon adobe buildings. He woke the vaqueros at one camp and a farm family at the second. His warning was the same...head for the Bustamante ranch within twenty-four hours.

Dawn was breaking as he reached the green, hilly area around the rancho. He noted that the outlying adobe huts were empty, an indication that his earlier warning had been heeded. Ricardo walked Oro up to the walled headquarters and was recognized by the guards and immediately admitted. The big doors swung open, and he rode into the courtyard and dismounted. Ricardo felt a deep weariness come over him as he walked behind the servant to his room. He left instructions to be awakened as soon as Don Carlos was prepared to see him. Then he fell on top of the bed into an immediate deep sleep.

It was nearly noon when he awoke. As he finished washing, a servant entered.

"I left orders to be awakened when Don Carlos got up," said Ricardo.

"Don Carlos said to let you sleep. He would like you to have lunch with him on the patio," the small man told Ricardo.

"Tell him I'll be there in a few minutes."

Ricardo used the next few minutes to clip his mustache and brush off his clothes. He felt a surge of excitement knowing that Maria was there. The thought of touching her, of feeling her warmth and talking to her made him wide awake.

He approached the small patio, which was surrounded with flowers and shrubs. Don Carlos was already there, and two servants stood discreetly in the background. Ricardo and Don Carlos embraced each other heartily.

"Welcome back. My home is yours," said the patron.

"I have missed you, and your lovely daughter," said Montoya.

"Maria is on my mind," said Bustamante. "Sit down, Ricardo. Let us talk."

They seated themselves and drank coffee. The rancher looked closely at Ricardo. "Because of the coming problems with the Apaches, do you recommend that I send her to Hermosillo to stay with my sister?"

Ricardo felt a sinking feeling in his stomach, but he tried to mask his disappointment. "I would strongly recommend it. She would be safe in a city." His stomach began to churn.

"When should I send her?"

"Immediately," said Ricardo. "They could begin raiding out of the mountains any day."

The older man sighed and nodded his head in understanding, but he could see that Ricardo was disappointed. "Why don't you accompany the party that takes her?" said Don Carlos. "It would please me to know that she is in your care."

Ricardo's spirits suddenly soared. "Of course, Don Carlos. It would be my pleasure to serve you."

They discussed the pending raids and how to prepare for them. Bustamante sent for a map of the ranch and surrounding areas. After studying and talking about the alternatives, Montoya recommended that Don Carlos send out three scouting parties, with eight men in each group. The rancher then summoned three vaqueros and asked them to lead the scouting parties.

Ricardo briefed them. "Each of your groups will scout the designated areas," he said, pointing to locations on the map. "At dusk you will split into two-man teams and spread out over the foothill territory you are assigned to cover. Find a good vantage point, stay hidden, and watch. The Apaches will move at night and usually attack in the early morning hours. As soon as it is light, each group will form up, cook, and sleep during the day only. When a team spots a war party, one of the two men should head for the ranch here, while the other gathers the scouts together."

Ricardo studied the three vaqueros and was satisfied that each was brave and intelligent enough to carry out the orders properly.

"How long will this continue?" one of the cowboys asked.

"As long as it takes. The federal rurales should arrive in two weeks or less. Their commander, Constantine Vorshoff, you have all heard of. His ideas on how to find and trap the Apaches are much like mine," said Ricardo.

Vorshoff was a legendary Russian cavalry officer whom the Mexican government had hired to combat the Apaches in the northern states of Sonora and Chihuahua. His successes had earned him the rank of general in the Mexican army, full citizenship, a huge salary, and a magnificent hacienda. He had decided not to return to Russia.

"The United States Cavalry has also followed the Apaches, but I fear they intend to follow the Indians into the mountains. It could mean disaster," Ricardo said. "We cannot count on the gringos for assistance."

On the map, Montoya outlined the scouting positions, base camps, and watering holes. The scouting groups were to be changed every week and fresh vaqueros brought in. The remainder of Don Carlos's men would be kept near the ranch for protection. They discussed the strategy for another half hour before the vaqueros left to organize their men.

Don Carlos excused himself, and Ricardo was alone when Maria Bustamante entered the patio. She was dressed in a long, pink flowery dress, which accented her soft complexion and long, dark hair. Maria smiled at Ricardo, and her dark eyes were soft and enchanting.

"I'm so glad you're back," she said, and touched his arm.

Ricardo looked around for her aunt, who followed Maria everywhere, and spotted the iron-jawed lady standing behind a climbing rose bush. Her fierce eyes and stiff bearing indicated no compromise would be granted and no quarter given in her mission to keep Maria away from men.

"I've missed you," said Ricardo quietly.

He wanted to reach out and touch her, to take her in his arms, to hold her. But instead they sat at the small table and talked quietly about where he had been and what he had learned about his ancestry. Aunt Anna was ever vigilant, unrelenting, and seemed to have ice water flowing in her veins.

"It is good being with you again," Maria said softly.

Ricardo looked disturbed. "There is something you should know. Your father thinks you would be safer in Hermosillo until the Apache situation is resolved. I agree.

You are to leave first thing in the morning. I will go along with the escort."

Maria was visibly upset. "I don't want to leave. This is my home."

Ricardo dropped his eyes. "It may not be for that long."

"And, then again, it might," she said quickly. "There have been other Apache raids. I never had to leave in the past. I don't think I should have to now."

"The number of Apaches is much greater this time," said Ricardo.

"They wouldn't attack here," she pointed out.

"It's a remote possibility, but it could happen," he argued.

She jumped to her feet. "You will excuse me!"

Maria went directly to her father, but her arguments were to no avail. He had decided that she would leave in the morning, and he would not change his mind.

The following morning the party set out early. Ricardo alternated between riding in the enclosed coach and scouting ahead on Oro. Aunt Anna sat next to Maria and across from Ricardo. Her piercing eyes never wavered as they stared at him, and Ricardo began to welcome the interludes when he was able to ride out ahead. Aunt Anna unnerved Montoya more than a confrontation with any adversary. She would grunt, rather than say yes or no, in response to his polite questions or observations about the countryside.

For a few moments, Ricardo would talk with Maria and admire her beauty and lithe figure. A glance at Aunt Anna and her sullen expression confirmed that she knew what he was thinking. He went from feeling uncomfortable to being distressed before he decided to remain on his horse for the last five miles of the trip.

Aunt Rosa and her husband, Luis Enriquez, had a beautiful home on the outskirts of Hermosillo, with tiered flower gardens and a magnificent view of the city. Enriquez was a vegetable farmer, and his holdings covered several thousand acres.

As usual, Aunt Anna followed Maria like a faithful dog, and Ricardo was not able to see her alone. That night he lay on his bed thinking that maiden aunts and rattlesnakes had about the same effect on him.

Montoya was in the barn saddling Oro the following morning when he heard a noise behind him. Maria was standing there and threw herself into his arms as he turned around. He was holding her, caressing her, and looking over her shoulder for Aunt Anna at the same time. Ricardo could sense that Maria was consumed with the same burning passion he was feeling. The rapture he felt being against her body transferred to sexual excitement and raw passion.

CHAPTER 11

The mountain range rose majestically against the early morning sky. Rugged peaks and valleys were shrouded in a blue-black haze. Foreboding and impenetrable, the Sierra Madres were everything the United States Army troopers had come to hate.

Early morning was the only cool time of day. The men clustered around a dozen small fires, drinking coffee and eating breakfast. Three Apache scouts materialized out of the surrounding rocks and approached Captain Beeshore. The Apaches used sign language and spoke some Spanish to Sergeant Kincaid. He nodded in understanding but looked skeptical.

"What did they say?" Beeshore demanded.

"Through that pass, the mountains flatten out and form a big valley where the 'paches are camped. That's what they tell me," said the leather-faced sergeant.

"What do you think?" asked Beeshore.

"I don't like it. Why would they let us get this close?" Kincaid mused. "Them scouts claim we can circle 'round this peak and come up behind them."

"Oh?" said Beeshore. "How long will it take?"

Kincaid talked with the scouts again. They looked similar to other Apaches, except for their blue Army shirts.

Kincaid turned back to Beeshore. "It'd take most of the day to walk around and over the foothills of this mountain. Can't ride horses, the terrain's too rough."

The red-faced captain weighed the pros and cons involved. He was a bitter man. Beeshore's wife had left him the year before, he had been passed over for promotion, and then he'd been transferred to the Arizona Territory, which was considered a dead end. There was little chance for glory chasing savages in a land that was hot, windy, and mountainous. Instead of being assigned to hunt down Cochise or Geronimo, the captain had been ordered to find Sky Walker and his group. Beeshore had no respect for the Apaches, believing them to be inferior to United States soldiers. He reasoned that they would run until caught and then surrender.

Beeshore scraped the skin from his peeling face and swore an oath. "All right, this is what we're going to do. Lieutenant Fredericks, I want you to take forty men and continue following along this route. I'll take the rest of the men and the scouts and circle around. At dusk tonight we'll attack from both angles."

Lieutenant Kenneth Fredericks remembered what Ricardo had told him. The young man was fresh out of West Point, where Indian tactics were not taught. But he was blessed with good common sense and the desire to listen and learn from more experienced men. He reasoned that Montoya knew what he was talking about, and shoved aside his reluctance to question Captain Beeshore's orders.

"I have a question, sir," said Fredericks.

"What is it?" growled Beeshore.

"Is it wise to split our force in hostile territory when we don't know exactly where our objective is?" said Fredericks.

Beeshore's red face turned scarlet. "Don't talk to me about tactics. You know nothing, absolutely nothing, about fighting the enemy. What I want you to do is try and follow orders, if that's within your capabilities."

"Yes, sir," said Fredericks.

Kincaid thought it was time for him to say something, even if it meant receiving the captain's wrath. "I'd think twice afore trustin' them 'paches."

Beeshore's eyes blazed. "Risk and daring are part of soldiering. You don't win without them. Sergeant, you stay behind with Lieutenant Fredericks. I don't want any timid souls with me."

The words stung Kincaid. He came to attention, saluted, and walked off.

Fredericks saw that further argument would be useless. "I'll see to splitting the force," he said, and moved toward the troopers.

Captain Beeshore and his troopers departed a half hour later. The men in blue slowly worked their way through the huge piles of boulders and around the side of the mountain. Fredericks thought they looked like ants as they scurried and scampered over and around the rock formations. They worked their way higher and finally out of sight.

Sergeant Kincaid approached the lieutenant. "Sir, I don't like it. Yellow Hand is heading them scouts. He's a treacherous one. Done more killin' of whites than the ones we're chasin'."

Fredericks studied his sergeant for a moment. "I may be green, but I'm not dumb. I'll want your advice every inch of the way as we progress," Fredericks told Kincaid.

Kincaid grinned. He liked the young lieutenant.

"I'll shore tell ya," said Kincaid.

Fredericks's men had a much shorter route to travel than the captain's. The lieutenant ordered six troopers up the mountains on each side of his loose formation. The men used binoculars to study the terrain. Travel was slow and methodical, but Fredericks wanted to make sure that no Apaches would be above them as they progressed. There was no stopping for lunch. The men ate beef jerky and bread as they continued progressing slowly. The rocky route they had been following gradually became narrower. Fredericks called a halt and talked with Kincaid.

"If you have suggestions, I want to hear them," said Fredericks.

Kincaid just shook his head. "I don't think this here trail's goin' anyplace."

Fredericks had a sinking feeling in his stomach. "Let's climb and take a look."

Fredericks and another trooper climbed upward for nearly an hour before the lieutenant reached the vantage point he was seeking. Below and in front of him he could see that the mountain slopes gradually came together to create a solid mass of rock that no group could penetrate. He descended swiftly.

"You're right," said Fredericks to Kincaid. "There is no passage. The scout lied."

Kincaid spit a stream of chewing tobacco. "That means they's gonna spring a trap on the captain."

"Let's get moving," Fredericks ordered.

Kincaid raised his hand. "Listen," he said.

What sounded like a low roll of thunder could be heard, and a feeling of dread passed over Fredericks.

***

Yellow Hand was a small, wiry warrior known for his quickness in combat. He had volunteered for the scouting mission out of boredom with reservation life. Yellow Hand hated the whites and reservation survival, and when he sensed that Sky Walker's men were watching, a plan formed in his mind. He had been alone and out in front of the group on the preceding afternoon when he had signaled the Chiricahuas that he wanted to parley. For the choice of two wives from among Sky Walker's band, he had agreed to lead the soldiers into an ambush.

Now he was leading the soldiers again. He came to the prearranged location where the trail led through a gorge with steep sides. Yellow Hand knew that the Apaches were hidden in the rocks on both sides of the gorge.

One of the other two scouts ran up to him as they started along the narrow path.

"Bad place," the tall Indian said.

Yellow Hand agreed but said that it was the only way through. He ignored the other Indian and raced along the path. The other scouts were inexperienced and followed reluctantly. The gorge was nearly a half mile long, and Yellow Hand kept up a fast pace over the small boulders and rocks strewn on the bottom of the gorge. As it widened and reached larger rock formations on the floor, Yellow Hand stopped. He waited for the second scout to catch up and then motioned him to pass. As the tall Indian moved past him, Yellow Hand drew his knife and leaped on the other man's back.

***

Captain Beeshore was midway back in the column of eighty-five men as it stretched in snakelike fashion along the narrow canyon. The first volley of gunfire from the Apaches made the cavalry troopers scurry around like frightened animals trying to hide in cracks in the walls or gain protection behind small rocks. Beeshore's mouth was wide open with surprise, which suddenly turned to dread as he realized that the Apaches were firing down from both sides. His men had little or no protection from the repeated gunfire, which echoed off the canyon walls.

"Shoot them! Shoot them!" Beeshore yelled.

He fired his rifle at puffs of smoke, but none of the shots found their mark. Ten troopers were killed in the first fusillade from the Apaches. Another five were wounded. The din of battle was magnified by the sheer rock walls, and smoke hung in the air, obscuring the cavalrymen's view.

Seconds passed and the firing became more intense. Beeshore yanked out his revolver and fired repeatedly without aiming. A rifle bullet smashed into the back of his head and he pitched forward onto his face.

**

Moments later, the soldiers became panicky, and a mass of blue-clad men began running back the way they had come. Now the Apaches stood up and fired at will. There were no return shots from the terrified and disorganized band of cavalrymen. They felt naked without their horses and had been led into an untenable position. Fear of what the Apaches would do to them if they were wounded and captured turned the race for survival into a headlong stampede. Troopers ran over the bodies of their fallen comrades, pushing and shoving as they raced back along the trail. Wounded men cried out for assistance. Others crawled or hobbled after the fleeing mass of blue coats. The Apaches calmly used the downed soldiers for target practice.

The retreating soldiers were packed closely together and made a large target for the Indians. The braves fired at the wall of blue coats and seldom missed. Troopers fell one after another, and their comrades did not even glance at their downed friends as they made their dash for survival.

Sergeant Bill Standish, a big, slow man, was at the rear of the column. When the firing had begun, he had lumbered back a short distance to the start of the canyon. Standish placed the troopers behind rocks as they came running out and had them direct their fire up at the positions held by the nearest Apaches. The diversionary fire helped pin down a few of the braves and made their shots less accurate.

Of the eighty-five troopers who walked into the gorge, only thirty made it out, and five of these men were wounded. They huddled behind the boulders and in crevices.

**

Sky Walker watched the carnage from his position high among the rocks overlooking the gorge. The ambush had worked perfectly. The bottom of the gorge was strewn with dead and dying soldiers, but the slaughter brought him no huge sense of satisfaction. Like other great leaders, he hated war and wanted peace for his people. This massacre, although a great victory for the Apaches, would bring the soldiers by the hundreds to hunt down his band. The white men always avenged a defeat at the hands of the Indians.

Three soldiers had managed to climb up the canyon wall at various locations and hide under rock outcroppings. The Apaches opposite them had only legs to shoot at and had been unable to dislodge them. The cavalrymen fired occasionally, but mainly just tried to stay out of sight.

"Shall I order the men to climb down and finish them?" Red Arrow asked.

Sky Walker pointed to the spots where the soldiers were hidden. "They must be killed first. Not one of our men should die when it is unnecessary."

"It may take time. Our braves must climb around the rocks until they can get better spots to shoot from," said Red Arrow.

Sky Walker looked impassively at his sub-chief. "Time we have. Braves to take the places of those wounded or killed, we don't."

Red Arrow said nothing, but Sky Walker knew he disagreed. Sooner or later Red Arrow would openly challenge his authority, and the break would come. Sky Walker pointed to areas on the canyon walls where he wanted the braves to descend in order to get better vantage points for shooting at the remaining soldiers.

"It will be dark soon," Red Arrow pointed out.

"Then it will be easier for our braves to collect the guns and boots from the dead soldiers. It can be done at night," said Sky Walker.

"Our men deserve to celebrate their victory in the daylight. They must be allowed to achieve victory in the sun," said Red Arrow in a loud voice.

"If you can kill the remaining white eyes without losing a brave, then do so," Sky Walker said reluctantly.

Red Arrow sprang into action. One of the soldiers was hidden below and to the right of where the chiefs were located. The sub-chief made his way rapidly down the canyon wall until he stood on the boulder that concealed the trooper. He kicked dirt and rocks down along one side of the boulder and then quickly climbed around the opposite side of the large rock. The young trooper was alerted by the falling pebbles, turned toward the disturbance, and raised his revolver to meet the expected enemy.

Red Arrow peeked around the opposite side of the rock, aimed his revolver, and put a bullet through the trooper's head. The youth's lifeless body tumbled down the wall of the gorge and fell among his comrades on the floor of the canyon. Red Arrow's victory cry echoed off the walls. He stood up, raised his revolver, and called to the spirits for victory. Other braves picked up the victory cry, and for a few minutes the canyon was filled with the eerie cries of the victorious warriors.

Other braves climbed down to the hiding places of the two remaining troopers. But these hunted soldiers were not as easy to kill. The first trooper shot one warrior through the chest and wounded a second before he died. The second blue coat shot one of the attacking Apaches in the leg, and the brave fell into the gorge. His head struck a rock, crushing his skull.

***

From the hollowed-out hole in the canyon wall, trooper John Drexel waited for the next Apache to appear.

But Sky Walker stood up and called to the warriors surrounding Drexel's sanctuary. They bypassed his hiding place and crawled down to the canyon floor. Drexel was to be the lone survivor from within the gorge.

He watched as the Apaches stripped the clothing and arms from his fallen comrades, and then scalped them. Drexel counted his remaining bullets and found that he had only eleven rounds left. He vowed to make each one count when they came for him. However, once the Apaches had taken everything of value, they proceeded up the canyon. Drexel had a bushy head of black hair and ran his hand through it, thinking grimly that he was the only white man around who could still accomplish that feat.

***

Sky Walker's band was laden with booty when they returned to camp. They now had a stock of guns and ammunition that would last them indefinitely. Three warriors had been wounded in the attack. The only two Apaches who had died had been killed in the assault on the hidden troopers.

The festivities in Sky Walker's camp that night lasted until daylight the following morning. He knew his people needed the joy that comes from victory in order to sustain them in the coming weeks and months. Sky Walker sensed that never again would his people attain success so easily. The Apache chief also knew that he would soon be challenged from within. Red Arrow was fast becoming the symbol of victory in Sky Walker's band. Many of the younger braves would follow Red Arrow regardless of the recklessness of his plans. Sky Walker was determined that no more of his people would die through needless confrontations with the whites. For most of the night, he prayed to the spirits for wisdom.

***

The following morning trooper John Drexel left the gorge and found Standish and his fellow survivors still on guard.

"How many are left besides you?" Standish asked.

The exhausted soldier slumped to the ground. "None."

Standish swallowed hard. "There must be others."

Drexel just shook his head. "There ain't. They're all dead. Every last one of them. I crawled into a hole in the wall of the canyon. It's the only reason I'm alive."

Drexel had stayed awake all night, fearing that the Apaches would try to sneak up on him in the darkness. As the morning dawned, he had looked down on the horrendous sight of his former companions being devoured by vultures. He shook his head at the gross stupidity of the whole venture.

The big sergeant looked angry. "I want to get them devils."

Drexel looked up at Standish. "If you go after them in there, you're goin' without me. I ain't never goin' back in them canyons."

From the far left side, one of the troopers yelled. Lieutenant Fredericks and his forty troops slowly made their way up the rocky slope to the mouth of the canyon. He dismounted and saluted Standish. The sergeant quickly told him what had occurred. Fifty-four men were dead.

Fredericks responded with surprising calm. He ordered Sergeant Kincaid to form up the men, take roll call, and see to their equipment prior to the long march back to the fort. Fredericks felt that the loss of his commanding officer and the death of nearly half the men necessitated his retirement from the field. His confidence had been badly shaken by the failure of the mission.

The lieutenant was discussing the condition of the wounded when suddenly another shout was heard from the advance guard. Framed in the sunlight as it came up over the low-lying eastern mountains was the tall vaquero on the golden horse. Montoya rode into their camp at a leisurely pace and swung down from his horse in front of Fredericks. Fredericks briefly explained what had occurred, but did not elaborate.

"What do you plan to do now?" Montoya asked.

"Go back to the fort," said Fredericks.

"Is this your decision or were prior orders issued?"

"It's my decision."

Montoya nodded his head in understanding. "I have a plan whereby we might be able to trap the Apaches. Are you interested?"

Fredericks looked at Kincaid.

"Ain't no way them men is goin' back in them gorges," said Kincaid quietly. "The fight's pretty well kicked outa them."

"This would involve fighting the Apaches in the open and on horseback," said Ricardo.

Kincaid's leathery face lit up. "Beggin' the lieutenant's pardon, but in that case, the men are ready."

Lieutenant Fredericks brightened up as he saw at least a slim chance to save his career, which seemed to have ended before it had even begun.

CHAPTER 12

During the next two weeks, Sky Walker's band sent only small raiding parties down out of the mountains to attack miners, traders, ranch-line camps, and families who lived on the outskirts of the small settlements in the area. Most of the raids were unsuccessful. Only three Mexicans had been caught and killed and a small amount of loot taken. The entire area at the base of the Sierra Madres had been alerted, and the massacre of the troopers only added to the vigilance of the populace. After such a resounding success, the Apache braves were hungry for more victories.

The Indians' base camp was at the end of a long canyon that opened into a huge meadow. The surrounding mountains were impenetrable, and no force could follow the Apaches through the pass without being butchered. A small spring provided water, and the food supply was large and varied. Each family lived in its own wickiup, a hovel of sticks and brush.

Red Arrow and three other sub-chiefs sat around the evening fire awaiting Sky Walker. The chief pushed aside the flap at the front of his wickiup, came out, and stood before the assembled leaders. He wore a multicolored blanket around his shoulders, and a cloth band of the same bright material circled his head, holding his long hair back.

Sky Walker's eyes were deep-set and expressionless. He appeared every inch the dominant leader as he took his place at the head of the group. His mouth was in a straight, fixed position, and he did not make his customary acknowledgements of the other sub-chiefs.

Red Arrow was the first to speak. "Our scouts tell us that the band of horses and the herd of cattle are still in the same location."

"It is true that we could use more horses, but there is no need for more beef," said Sky Walker.

The hawk-nosed sub-chief continued insistently. "Twice our scouts have traveled the entire area. There are only the six Mexicans who live in the small camp. We feel it is time to attack."

"Who is 'we'?" Sky Walker asked. He looked at Red Arrow for the first time.

Red Arrow returned Sky Walker's gaze. "The young fighting men."

"It is a trap," said Sky Walker. "There is no reason for them to be there."

"Our scouts can find no sign of other Mexicans. It would be a great honor to bring back the horses," Red Arrow emphasized.

"It is not wise to send out a large raiding party into the flat lands," Sky Walker said.

"There are many of us who feel it should be done," Red Arrow said loudly.

Little Hawk, another of the sub-chiefs, said, "Our young men are restless. They cannot stay here forever."

"Would you rather live on the reservation?" Sky Walker retorted sharply.

"My meaning was that the braves must be allowed to stalk the whites. It is our way of life," said Little Hawk.

Sky Walker looked first at one Apache and then at another. "We have had a great victory. It was achieved through patience. When cunning is replaced by recklessness, death will surely follow."

"There are those of us who do not agree," said Red Arrow.

Sky Walker looked fiercely at Red Arrow. "You are a brave warrior. But you are a fool. You sacrifice the lives of the braves when there is no need for it. A good leader always thinks first of the safety of his people."

The words stung Red Arrow. The insult had been hurled, and he was now humiliated in front of his peers. His eyes blazed. "I take offense at your words," he said quietly.

Sky Walker ignored the sub-chief and addressed the entire group. "We set out to be free. We are. We sought a safe refuge. We have one. We wanted full stomachs for our wives and children. They are well fed. We are living the lives we want to live. But this is not enough. You men listen to a hothead and want to take foolish risks."

A smoldering fury was bubbling up from deep within Red Arrow. "To be young is to be brave. The older a man gets, the sooner it is until he sits with the squaws."

No emotion crossed Sky Walker's noble face. His broad forehead, strong nose, and long face were every inch the features of a warrior chieftain. He rose to his feet.

"Let those who agree with me stand up," Sky Walker said loudly.

There was a moment's silence. Only Sitting Bear got to his feet. The other sub-chiefs stayed seated and would not look at Sky Walker.

A look of triumph flashed over Red Arrow's face. "The men have spoken," he stated with a note of finality in his voice.

"There cannot be two leaders in a band. We must live with a singleness of purpose," said Sky Walker.

Red Arrow got to his feet, expecting Sky Walker to say he and his family and friends would depart. But instead he pulled away his robe and revealed the body paintings of an Apache who was about to enter into combat.

"Red Arrow, before you can lead the Chiricahuas, you must prove you are fit," said Sky Walker.

The sub-chief looked surprised, and then his expression turned to one of eager anticipation. He was sure he could kill Sky Walker in a knife fight. Sky Walker was over forty, while Red Arrow was twenty-five. Red Arrow also thought he was faster and stronger and could conquer any brave in the band.

The Indians in camp quickly built their fires higher until the center of the clearing was a mass of flickering shadows and light. The two combatants stood opposite one another while the medicine man performed the expected rituals and chanting.

The physical contrast between the two men was striking. Red Arrow was a head shorter than the older chief, barrel-chested, with huge arms and big legs. His square, block like face, hook nose, and piercing eyes gave him a ferocious, ruthless look.

Sky Walker was tall and dignified. His strong features and noble bearing projected the image of a born leader. He was a tall, strong man, but he did not look like a man who relished fighting. It had been two years since Sky Walker had actually led war parties, and most of the younger braves had never seen him fight. Some of the old men had seen him in action, but none of them had left the reservation with this band. The young men around camp respected his wisdom and experience, but they imagined that Red Arrow would certainly be the winner.

The chief of the Chiricahua band had tolerated Red Arrow's rebellious attitude until they reached the safety of the Sierra Madres. He had wanted no internal struggles until the band had reached its destination. Sky Walker was blessed with patience, and it had served him well. Now it was time for him to prove once again that he was worthy of being chief. Sky Walker was still young enough that he had to accept challenges rather than rule from the position of elder statesman. Traditionally, no brave would challenge a chief, because the rank was an inherited one. But the times dictated a necessity for change. Geronimo was not a chief, yet his aggressive behavior and successful raids against the whites had gained him a following. Red Arrow believed he should lead as well.

The rituals were completed, the command to begin was given, and the two men circled each other. Each carried a tomahawk and knife. They were stripped to the waist, and each was marked with yellow and black war paint. There was absolute silence from the band, who had all gathered in a large circle to view the battle.

The combatants thrust and parried with the knives, and slashed and blocked with the tomahawks. Red Arrow was the aggressor. He was continually moving forward, while Sky Walker moved sideways and backward.

The challenger rushed Sky Walker and brought his tomahawk downward in a long arc. The chief ducked and moved straight toward the oncoming body, then lifted Red Arrow and threw him over his shoulder. The muscular brave landed hard but, like a cat, was on his feet again in an instant. He returned to the attack, always advancing. Red Arrow's eyes glittered in the firelight as he stalked his prey. Sky Walker's eyes were alert and continually moving, anticipating his adversary's strategy.

Red Arrow dived forward and slashed with his knife. Its razor edge cut across Sky Walker's left thigh and blood flowed down over his entire leg. In response, Sky Walker slashed with his tomahawk and caught Red Arrow with a glancing blow on his back. But the blade did not strike a straight blow, and the wound was shallow.

Again Red Arrow lunged forward, meaning to drive his knife blade into Sky Walker's stomach. The chief side-stepped and hooked Red Arrow's foot with his own.

The challenger was tossed and landed with his right side in one of the fires. He screamed in agony as he brushed the blazing wood from his back. Throwing all caution to the wind, he rushed Sky Walker, but the chief continued to back away, jumping from side to side, parrying blows, and continually retreating.

During the next few moments, they moved in a tighter and tighter circle, their chests heaving from the exertion as they gasped for air. Red Arrow feinted to his left and then thrust his right arm forward. The knife blade penetrated Sky Walker's left side. The chief dropped his tomahawk and grabbed Red Arrow's wrist, falling backward onto the ground and at the same time pulling his body free of the knife. The challenger sensed that victory was his and jumped on the chief to end his struggles. Sky Walker jabbed upward with his knife just as Red Arrow's weight landed on him. His knife blade went into Red Arrow's throat, and the brave's eyes widened as his mouth opened to choke out his final breath.

Sky Walker thrust his dying opponent off to one side and climbed to his feet. Blood was streaming from his side and leg wounds, but he walked by himself to his wickiup, where he was treated by the medicine man. The Apache band talked loudly in disbelief at the outcome, which few had expected. Red Arrow's squaw began to wail in the background.

The following morning Sky Walker lay in his wickiup, close to death from loss of blood. If he survived, it would be many days before he could again lead his people. Little Raven was chosen by the sub-chiefs to lead the band until Sky Walker recovered. Little Raven was a small brave, but a veteran of many battles against the enemy in Mexico and the Arizona Territory. He respected Sky Walker and would never attempt to challenge his authority when he was the leader. But Little Raven was now the substitute leader, and like any chief, he intended to have his way. He chose to follow the path that Red Arrow would have taken, believing that the cattle and horses should be taken as prizes. Because he had been in the scouting party, he had seen the white stallion in the band of horses and wanted it for his own.

Upon hearing that Little Raven was to take the men and follow Red Arrow's plan, Sky Walker called the sub-chiefs to him. He was weak and could barely whisper his wishes to them.

"Those of you who respect me and my leadership will stay here and not join this venture, for it is doomed. I have seen it in the stars," Sky Walker said in a faint voice.

Little Raven stepped forward. "The young fighting men have decided to follow me. Victory will be ours."

Sky Walker looked up at Little Raven. "Leave me," he said.

Little Raven stalked out of the wickiup and called for a meeting of the braves.

At the conclusion of the meeting, eighteen warriors led by Sitting Bear decided to stay with Sky Walker and honor his wishes. The other fifty-two warriors cast their fate with the interim chief.

"We will ride tonight and attack the Mexican cowboys at first light," said Little Raven.

From his wickiup, Sky Walker heard them depart and prayed to the spirits that he might be wrong.

***

Once they reached the flat country, the war party divided into three groups, with the bands on the right and left ordered to scout the area as best they could before daylight. The central group went to the area where the horses and cattle were located. Little Raven sent one brave up as close to the adobe line camp as he could go. An hour before daylight the scout reported back and said that only a few vaqueros were in the hut.

"They have dogs. It will not be possible to surprise them," he told Little Raven.

The other two groups reached the rendezvous point on schedule and reported no trace of additional Mexicans. Satisfied that all was well, Little Raven deployed his men. As the first streaks of light shone in the sky, they struck.

Nearly two dozen braves attacked the bunk house, while the remainder proceeded to drive off the herds of cattle and horses. As expected, the dogs did alert the vaqueros, who poured a deadly return fire at the Apaches. The braves rushed the main door of the adobe building, but were unable to force their way inside. Six braves were killed during the attack, and the main group fell back and took cover.

Suddenly, to the east, a large group of Mexicans came into view. Little Raven recognized their leader, the tall man on the golden horse. He signaled his braves to leave the cattle and horses and make a run at the vaqueros, who were blocking their return to the sanctuary of the mountains. The braves closed ranks and smashed into the line of Mexicans, who were riding full tilt to meet them. Gunfire echoed across the prairie land as the Indians rushed the Mexican cowboys. Blazing guns took their toll on each side as more than a dozen Apaches were shot off their horses and an equal number of Mexicans went down.

***

For the close fighting, Ricardo used his revolver and shot two Apaches. He then pulled Oro around and followed the Apache band as they raced back to the mountains. The pursuing Mexicans sent a roaring burst of gunfire into the retreating Chiricahuas, who were tightly bunched together as they fled. Another five Apaches and three horses were hit and went down. The braves who were unseated and wounded were forced to stand their ground, and went down under heavy gunfire as the Mexicans rode over them.

Twenty-eight Apache braves were still mounted and riding hard when they ran headlong into Lieutenant Frederick's massed cavalry. The troopers had been waiting for the Indians at the foothills and greeted them with a fusillade of gunfire, which boomed and echoed back into the mountains.

Bullets from more than sixty rifles took down half the braves and brought their retreat to a grinding halt. The confused braves broke and headed in every direction, panic-stricken. The pursuing vaqueros continued their firing and joined with the cavalry to pursue the remnants of the Apache band.

Of the ten Apaches who reached the mountains, only three would live to return to camp. The other seven were pursued too closely to escape. Little Raven was shot through the back, one of the last to be killed.

Lieutenant Fredericks and his men were overjoyed at the success of Ricardo Montoya's plan. They'd had to wait in hiding for days, but patience had paid off. The young lieutenant was flushed with victory as he talked with Ricardo.

"Mr. Montoya, your tactics were brilliant, simply brilliant. I've learned more from you about fighting the Apaches than I have from all the military books ever written," he blurted out.

Ricardo was smiling. "Give yourself some credit, Lieutenant. Few officers would have kept their commands in the field after such a disastrous defeat."

Fredericks grinned. "I didn't have much choice. If I'd gone back after Captain Beeshore's debacle, my career would have been finished. I'd have had to resign my commission."

"But it wasn't your fault."

"That doesn't matter. Someone in charge has to take the blame," said Fredericks.

Montoya shook his head. "It's a strange way to run an army."

"It's the United States 'way'," said Fredericks.

The two men looked at each other, and the absurdity of the statement struck home. A deep blush crept over Frederick's face, and a moment or two passed before both men began laughing.

Ricardo's plan had been simple. He had deployed his Mexican scouts in the mountain foothills. After the Apache raiding parties had passed the outposts as they ventured out onto the prairie, the scouts had made wide circles around the Indians and warned Ricardo and the cavalry, who had ridden to their designated attack points to await the strike. Everything had hinged on Montoya's belief that the Apaches would not pass up the opportunity to take the horses and cattle.

Fredericks and Montoya drank coffee beside a small fire while the wounded were being treated.

"What's your guess as to the number of Apaches still in the hills?" Fredericks asked.

Ricardo thought for a moment. "Maybe twenty who aren't wounded. They'll be busy all the time trying to get food and supplies for a hundred women and children. We will continue to keep scouts in the foothills. The Indian raiding parties will be much smaller, and they will have to conduct numerous raids. It will be much easier to catch them. They may escape many times, but sooner or later we will destroy them."

Fredericks threw the remaining coffee from his cup into the fire. "What will happen to them?"

"In time, they will surrender and be sent back to the reservation," said Ricardo.

"If they weren't such barbarous devils...." Fredericks said, his words trailing off.

Ricardo knew what he was thinking. "Yes. They have no real place to call home. They have been driven from their lands and forced to live like dogs. When they resist, we kill them."

CHAPTER 13

During the next few weeks, Ricardo remained in the hills to coordinate the activities of the vaqueros from the larger ranchos as they defended themselves against the Apache raids. The Indians were more skillful in eluding both the scouts' early detection and ensuing counterattacks, but their rewards were meager. They were able to kill only three farmers, and returned to the mountains with a small amount of food and supplies. The mountains had become both a fortress and a prison to the Indians.

Montoya left the defensive forces and rode back to Don Diego Salazar's ranch. He was drawn back to the hacienda where he had spent his childhood, had risen to high rank, and had spent so many pleasant years. He leaned against a tree and looked across the rolling hills to the white buildings that rose majestically from the center of the panoramic view. As always, the ranch headquarters, less than a mile away, drew him like a magnet.

Ricardo was lost in thought. His mind went to his father, Gustavo. He smiled as he thought of the many happy times his close family had had together. His smile changed to a frown as his thoughts turned to the Barringers. *How can I be someone named James Barringer? Must I go back?*

He thought of the woman in the picture, his real mother. Such a beautiful woman. Such a tragedy. His mind focused on John Barringer, and he spat on the ground. Then Victoria Barringer came into his mind. Ricardo smiled and shook his head. He was amazed by her elegance, dignity, grace, and total command of every situation she encountered.

Rafael Montoya rode up and dismounted, and the two brothers greeted each other warmly.

"How goes it, Rafael?" Ricardo asked.

Rafael took off his sombrero and wiped his brow. "Not good. Don Diego has placed a reward of twenty-five thousand pesos on your head. I am being watched. He learned that you were behind the plan to catch the Apaches. It made him furious to think that he was supplying men to work under your command."

"You know I never went near the Salazar riders. Someone else always carried information to them," said Ricardo.

"I know, I know. But the truth got back to Don Diego. He even accused me of being involved. He's acting more and more like a crazy man. I think he fears you. Fears that you will ride up some day and take everything away from him," said Rafael.

Ricardo thought for a moment and then lit a cigar. He looked at his brother. "There is only one thing for me to do, and that is to leave Mexico for a while. I have business in Arizona anyway."

The brothers talked briefly about the Barringers and what had transpired.

"Is this John Barringer the type who would kill his own brother?" Rafael asked, a worried look in his eye.

Ricardo thought for a few seconds. "That's an accusation that cannot be made without proof. I'm going back to find out one way or another."

"What's to keep him from trying to murder you again?"

"He wouldn't do it on the ranch. His mother—my grandmother—controls everything and everyone."

Rafael grinned. "She must be one grand woman."

"She is," Ricardo replied.

Rafael had a mischievous look on his face. "Are your feet still off the ground over Maria Bustamante?"

Ricardo looked embarrassed. "We still see each other."

Over the past few weeks, Ricardo had infrequently returned to Hermosillo. Every hour he spent with Maria was grand and glorious, and he rode back into the mountains only with deep regret. He dreaded telling her that he must return to the Arizona Territory once more.

Rafael knew his brother well. "Will I hear church bells in the near future?"

Ricardo laughed. "Now is not the time."

His brother nodded in agreement and frowned. "Lupe wants to set a date soon, but until things straighten themselves out, who knows?"

"I'm sorry, Rafael. I know it's mostly my fault," said Ricardo.

"Don't blame yourself. Don Diego acts so crazy, anything could set him against me or anyone else," Rafael replied. "When do you leave?"

"I'll ride to the Bustamante ranch tonight. Tomorrow or the next day I'll leave for Arizona."

Rafael laughed. "Or the next, or the next, or when she lets you go."

Ricardo tackled his brother, and they rolled around on the grass like children.

***

Upon his return to the Bustamante ranch, Ricardo conferred with Don Carlos in his library. His daughter had returned from Hermosillo.

"There is no great fear for the safety of the people on the rancho anymore. Just keep your men ready to ride when the scouts learn of Apache movements," Ricardo instructed the ranch owner.

"I will," said Bustamante. He observed Ricardo closely. "Are you leaving us again?" he asked quietly.

"With regret," said Ricardo. "I have unfinished business involving the Barringer family."

Don Carlos was saddened by the news, although he had expected it. "You are very intense, Ricardo. It is both good and bad. It drives you to great accomplishments, but it often leaves you in peril."

"There are things I must find out."

The silver-haired rancher studied Ricardo. "And then what? More killing? In the end, will you achieve anything?"

"My mind will be clear," he said in an unconvincing voice.

"I'll not try to tell you your business, except to say that living in the present is more important than trying to discover the past," said Bustamante.

"The honorable thing is to go back and find the killer," said Montoya. "It is something even you would do."

"Not with so many years gone by. Or perhaps I look at things differently now that I'm older and have a family," said Don Carlos.

There was a knock on the door and Maria entered, followed by Aunt Anna. Ricardo's heart leaped when he saw the beautiful woman—and plummeted as Aunt Anna fixed him with her ice-cold stare. Maria kissed her father on the cheek and turned to Ricardo.

"I'm so happy you're back," she said brightly. "Let's walk on the patio."

Ricardo looked at Don Carlos, who nodded his approval. Ricardo took Maria by the arm, and they walked from the room. Aunt Anna stalked across the room at the heels of her ward, intending to continue her relentless watch over the young maiden's virtue.

"Anna," said Bustamante.

The square-jawed, powerfully built woman whirled around and looked sharply at her brother. "I must be with her at all times."

"Not today," said Don Carlos. "Let them be alone."

Aunt Anna's eyes widened, and she looked horrified at the thought. "Ever since your beloved wife died, I have looked after Maria. I have always done what is right for her."

Don Carlos sighed and rolled his eyes. "My gratitude is undying. Your energy and enthusiasm are unquestioned. But now is not the time."

"I must protest—"

"Your protest is noted, but my wish is that they be alone today," he said.

Aunt Anna's eyes blazed. She gave the patron a look that indicated he was betraying his daughter, then turned angrily and left the room.

If only she weren't so enthusiastic, thought Don Carlos.

***

Ricardo and Maria spent most of the day relaxing and enjoying each other's company. They walked among the flower gardens, took an afternoon ride, and later watched as the vaqueros broke some wild mustangs. That evening a lavish banquet was prepared in honor of Ricardo. Bustamante, his family members, and the ranch overseers all drank toasts to Ricardo. Mariachis serenaded Ricardo and Maria.

Later that evening, they were finally alone in the large living room. She was in his arms, and he blocked everything else from his mind. Lust and his desire to possess Maria took over. He kissed her passionately and she gasped as his hands moved over her body. She became aroused, sensuous, and wanted Ricardo.

"Don't ever leave me again," she whispered. He suddenly stiffened, and she sensed something was wrong. "What is it?" she asked.

"I have to go back to Arizona one more time."

She pulled herself away from him. "You can't. That place isn't for you. Don't you want to stay with me?"

"I want to be with you more than anything. But I must go back."

Maria suddenly felt her world crumbling. "It's crazy. The whole thing is crazy. You're Mexican, just as I am. Can't you give up such nonsense?"

"No, I can't. I'm leaving tomorrow, because to prolong it won't do either of us any good."

Maria looked defiantly into his eyes. "I can't accept this."

"Maria, when I come back next time, it will be to stay."

She stepped backward, away from him. "Don't make any promises you don't intend to keep."

"What do you mean?"

"I mean, I don't intend to wait for a man who cares so little about his life. I don't think you'll come back. Those people will kill you."

"Now it's you who's being silly—" Ricardo stopped talking as a house servant entered the room.

"My apologies, but a man is here to see you," said the peon.

Maria turned and left the room. Ricardo walked out into the courtyard.

"Hello, Manuel," he said to the rider, who had come from the Salazar ranch.

"Ricardo, Don Diego has stripped Rafael of rank and imprisoned him at the ranch. He was followed when he met with you last time," said the vaquero.

"Is there any chance you were followed?"

"None. Rafael got word to me to come here and tell you. I owe a great deal to Rafael. It was my pleasure to serve him," said Manuel.

"We appreciate your friendship. Let us take different routes back, so that no one will connect us," said Ricardo.

The vaquero nodded his agreement.

Fifteen minutes later, Montoya was on the main trail leading to the Salazar ranch. Again Ricardo was frustrated and disappointed that Maria could not accept him for the man he was. *Will my love for Maria end in happiness*? He thought.

***

Rafael had returned to the rancho and immediately been summoned to Don Diego's office. Salazar, as usual, was dressed in matching ornate black silk jacket and trousers. He sat in a high-backed chair that dwarfed the slender man. His feet were propped up on the desk, and he tapped his fingers together as he surveyed Rafael, watching him much as a cat would view a cornered mouse. His small black eyes glared at Rafael, and his thin lips were pinched together under his neatly clipped mustache.

"Where have you been?" Salazar demanded loudly.

A guard stood on either of Salazar. Both men had their hands resting on their revolvers. Rafael sensed that Don

Diego knew he had returned from a meeting with Ricardo. He decided to play it straight.

"I met with my brother."

Salazar jumped to his feet. His face reddened, and his pointed beard moved up and down as his chin quivered. "You met with my enemy! I had you followed," he shouted.

"That's what I said," Rafael replied.

"Ricardo Montoya is wanted. There is a reward for him. He is my enemy. Yet you snuck off and met with him. I knew I couldn't trust a Montoya. I knew it!" Salazar yelled.

The ranch owner was working himself into one of his famous frenzies. Both Ricardo and Rafael had acted as buffers in the past and had often lessened the impact of his tirades. But there was no one to do so now.

"How could you have betrayed me after all I've done for you?" asked Salazar. His eyes were wide with fury as he awaited the answer.

"A man's brother will be his brother," said Rafael. "I have served you well and protected you many times, Don Diego. It was not in my mind to betray you, only to talk with my brother."

"You lie! You're plotting to kill me. You and that traitorous brother of yours. How could I have been so deceived?" said Salazar.

The rancher was gasping for breath, his face red and his eyes wide. Rafael knew it was useless to talk, so he remained quiet.

"Take his gun!" Don Diego ordered.

One of the guards walked forward and disarmed Rafael.

"Lock him in the small room adjacent to the storehouse," Salazar ordered.

Don Diego and Rafael regarded each other with mixed feelings for a brief moment. Salazar suddenly realized he was alone without a trusted adviser. Rafael's climb to power was over, and the downward fall had been swift and complete. In a perverse way, the two men had relied on each other, but the pact was broken. Rafael left.

"Luis!" Don Diego yelled.

A short, fat vaquero hurried into the room. Luis Cabrillo had slits for eyes, long bushy eyebrows, and a thin mustache that stretched across his fat face. He wore two bandoleers, broad cartridge belts crisscrossing his chest. It was difficult to perceive what Cabrillo was thinking because his eyes were so deeply recessed. He was the latest of Don Diego's promotions.

"I want this place guarded like it's never been guarded before. I know he'll come for his brother. I know it! I know it!" Salazar shouted.

"The Montoyas have many friends among the vaqueros," Cabrillo said in a deep, hoarse voice.

"Yes. What are you getting at?"

"Perhaps you should speak to the men. Let them know where they stand if they should collaborate with the enemy. There are too many like Rafael, who sneak around behind your back," Cabrillo said

"Yes. You're right. Assemble the men," he ordered.

Twenty minutes later, more than a hundred of Salazar's bodyguards and vaqueros stood at attention before the patron. Salazar had a whip in his hand, which he rapped loudly against his leg. His dark eyes shifted quickly from side to side as he reviewed the men.

"Let it be understood that Ricardo and Rafael Montoya are enemies, my enemies, from this day forth. Not one of you is to talk with them. No one is to help them in any way. If anyone meets with them secretly, he will be considered a traitor and will be shot!" Salazar shouted.

He waited for his words to sink in, and then continued. "Too many of you have helped Ricardo when you knew there was a price on his head. If I ever suspect any of you are helping him, or have seen him and not told me, then it is the end of you."

Salazar paced up and down before the front line of his vaqueros.

"Ricardo will come for his brother, who is locked up here," Salazar said, and pointed to the storehouse. "When he does, you men will kill him."

He stopped walking and studied the vaqueros. No one would meet his eyes.

"That is all!" Don Diego announced.

The men broke ranks and left the courtyard. Cabrillo followed Don Diego back inside.

"Well?" asked Salazar.

"They will cooperate now," Cabrillo stated.

***

Ricardo ran up to one of the rear walls of the fortress-like ranch house. He climbed up on a nearby adobe building and threw the grappling hook over the wall. Slowly, he pulled the rope back until the hook caught on top of the wall. He tested it with his full weight. It held. Having lived there for so long and supervised the protective screen of guards for the hacienda, Ricardo knew both its strengths and weaknesses.

He climbed the rope, pulled himself over the wall, stood on the balcony, and listened. Everything was quiet in the early-morning hours. He pulled up the rope and took the grappling hook with him, depositing it in the first storage shed he came to. Montoya had been able to bypass the guard posts with ease. The sentries were not as observant as they should have been, simply because there was no danger from outside attack and hadn't been for years. He noted that some were asleep.

Silently and swiftly, Ricardo climbed the side of the main building up to Don Diego's second-floor quarters. There were hand and footholds in the ornate architecture, making it fairly simple.

Ricardo climbed through the open window into the office. He froze as he realized a man was sitting in a chair not six feet from him. The guard gave out a soft snore, andRicardo walked quietly past him and opened the bedroom door. The door creaked, and he stopped, but the guard went on snoring. Ricardo waited a moment and then entered the large bedroom.

Against the far wall was a huge canopied bed. Moonlight came through the shuttered windows, casting strips of light across the large bed. Don Diego was restless and turned over on his back.

Montoya took out his knife and stood over the landowner. A slight smile came to his lips as he bent down and placed the flat part of the blade against Salazar's throat. Instantly, Don Diego's eyes flew open and he made a frightened, gasping noise. His mouth dropped open, and his terrified eyes were fixed on Ricardo's face.

"Hello, Don Diego."

Salazar moaned. "Don't kill me, please."

"I ought to slit your throat from ear to ear for what you've done to me and my family," Ricardo said quietly.

A deep groan came from Salazar again. Beads of sweat rolled down his forehead. "Please," he croaked.

"Now listen to me," said Ricardo as he put pressure on the knife blade. "If you do exactly what I say, you'll live. If you don't…." He made the motion of a throat being cut.

"Anything!" Don Diego pleaded.

Ricardo lifted the knife, and Don Diego's body relaxed into a pool of sweat. Montoya yanked back the cover and grabbed the small man by the arm, pulling him out of the bed. Ricardo put his knife away and pulled his revolver.

"We're going to walk down and release Rafael. You just keep telling the guards as we go by them not to do anything unless you give the order. Remember, if one of them shoots, you die," Ricardo explained.

"All right, all right. Let me get dressed," said Salazar.

"That won't be necessary. Just put on your robe."

"But I won't be dressed in front of the guard!"

"They won't mind," said Montoya.

"Please, Ricardo."

Montoya picked up a robe from a nearby chair and flung it at the patron. Salazar quickly put it on.

They walked into the next room where the guard slept. Ricardo kicked him in the leg, and the vaquero jumped to his feet and reached for his revolver.

"No!" Don Diego ordered. "Leave your gun alone."

The guard recognized Ricardo.

"Walk ahead of us and warn the other guards not to do anything," said Ricardo. "Isn't that right, Don Diego?"

"Yes, yes," the frightened rancher said. "Do as he says. Tell the men not to do anything unless I give the command. Is that clear?"

"Yes," the Mexican cowboy said. He knew that he was in a lot of trouble for sleeping on the job, and in even more trouble for letting Montoya get to Salazar.

The guard walked ahead of them down the hallway and then down the stairs that led to the main part of the house. He called to the other guards and repeated Salazar's warning. Ricardo and the barefoot rancher, his skinny legs protruding from the robe, moved at a rapid pace out into the courtyard, where guards were lighting torches and lanterns.

"Do what he says!" Don Diego yelled. "No one is to touch his gun."

They walked to the room that was used as a jail. Just before they reached the door, Don Diego yelled as he stepped on a sharp rock. He hopped on one foot and limped along the last few feet. A guard unbolted the door, entered, and helped Rafael get up from the bed.

Rafael yawned and squinted as he walked out of the building. He looked at the pathetic sight of Salazar bent over holding his sore foot. Then he noticed Ricardo. The two brothers began to laugh. Humiliated, Salazar dropped his head and stared at the ground. His pride and dignity were gone.

"Are you all right?" Ricardo asked his brother.

"The food could be better."

"Bring three horses," Ricardo ordered.

A few minutes later the three men were mounted. Don Diego's thin legs and bare feet hung from beneath his robe, giving him a birdlike appearance. The members of his bodyguard had worked with both Montoya brothers for years, and none of them even appeared interested in stopping the escape. Most were too busy suppressing their laughter as they looked at Salazar.

***

A young man watched the proceedings from one of the doorways. The look on his face was sly, calculating. Francisco Salazar viewed his father with hatred and loathing, even when he was in such a compromising position. *Kill him, you fools*, he thought to himself. *Do us all a favor.*

***

"Don Diego will be released once we are clear of the hacienda. No one is to follow," said Ricardo.

He took Salazar's reins and the three men rode out of the courtyard. Some of the vaqueros began laughing aloud. Others were more serious, knowing that Don Diego's wrath would be great when he returned.

It was daylight when they stopped. Salazar looked suspiciously at Ricardo. The landowner measured others' responses and motives against his own, and there was no charity or compassion in his spectrum of human emotions.

Ricardo studied Salazar. He noted that lines were showing in the once-smooth face. The patron was aging rapidly. Ricardo wondered what had caused the deterioration in mind and body. In a way, he almost felt sorry for the man he had helped achieve the pinnacle of success. Salazar was only a shell of the man he had once been.

As if he could read Ricardo's mind, Don Diego straightened up and his eyes flashed. "What is it you intend to do with me?" he stated loudly.

"I should put an end to your misery. It would be good for both of us," Ricardo said.

Salazar squinted at Montoya and seemed to shrink physically as fear swept over him.

Rafael sat quietly on his horse watching the two men. "Patron, you will not be harmed if you agree to leave us alone. That's all we want, to live our lives in peace."

"Of course! Of course! Anything!" Don Diego blurted out. "Just name it, and it's yours."

Neither brother believed him.

Ricardo's eyes bore into the landowner. "If you ever send men after us again, I'll come for you and end this feud."

"It ends here," Salazar assured them.

Both men knew he was lying.

"Go," said Ricardo.

Don Diego urged his horse forward. He was a laughable figure as he galloped away, his robe flapping about his thighs.

LEE BISHOP

CHAPTER 14

Sky Walker's strength gradually returned during the next few weeks. Once again he was the undisputed leader of his people, and there were no more challenges from the two dozen remaining braves. The chief continued to send out small scouting parties, but their successes were limited. The Apache band, which now contained four times more women and children than men, was having a difficult time feeding itself. The Mexicans were faster than ever in their response to the Indians' thefts of cattle and corn, and Sky Walker did not have the number of men necessary to carry out large-scale raids. The general mood in camp was one of dejection. Three out of four squaws had lost their husbands.

Sky Walker gathered the men to discuss alternatives. They sat in a circle as they talked.

"Two braves will be sent back to the reservation to make it known that Apaches willing to accept the families of those killed will be welcome to join us," said Sky Walker. "There should be many who are willing to come." The chief looked at the men gathered around him. Many nodded their assent.

"But this doesn't solve our main problem at the moment. We need food, especially vegetables and fruit. We have many mouths to feed. The Mexicans have pulled farther and farther back from the mountains. We have to go long distances, leaving ourselves open to ambush and attack." He paused to let his words sink in. "We could surrender the women and children to the Mexicans to be taken back to the reservation. This would include all the families without men," Sky Walker pointed out. "How many are in favor of this?"

The warriors looked around at one another. No one spoke up.

"Then, you feel as I do. No one should be forced back to the reservation. Also, there is no reason to believe that they would be returned alive," the chief said. "There is another way. South of us and to the west are the barrancas, as the Mexicans call the canyons that lead to the great ocean. There are many small towns close to the mountains. Raiding would be easier and more profitable. The problem is getting there."

Sitting Bear spoke up. "Have you seen this country?"

"Many years ago. Once, when I was young, I was taken as a slave and made to work the crops. I escaped and came back north," said Sky Walker.

"We cannot stay here. There's not enough food and few places to raid," said Sitting Bear.

Sky Walker surveyed his fighting men and noted that many agreed with Sitting Bear. "It is not as easy as it sounds," said the chief. "We would have to travel through the foothills, and our movements might be discovered. Also, once we go south, there are many Mexican army troops. The barrancas lead from the mountains to the sea, and would provide our enemies the opportunity to cut us off from our escape routes."

The Indians continued to discuss this plan for the next few hours. They finally voiced their individual opinions, and the vast majority was in favor of the move away from the ranches and toward the villages to the immediate south.

The remainder of the day was spent in preparation, and that night the trek began. The band stayed high in the foothills as they slowly picked their way south. The rocky terrain of the foothills prevented the procession from covering more than twenty miles the first night, so they climbed into the mountains and slept during the day. Scouts surprised two miners and brought the victims back to camp. They were questioned in Spanish and then put to death.

Satisfied that their exodus had not been discovered, Sky Walker allowed the Apaches to travel on flatter land the second night, and they reached their destination without mishap.

It took nearly a week before Sky Walker found the exact location he wanted. The new camp was located higher in the Sierra Madres, ringed with tall mountains. It provided three or four avenues of escape through canyons and over portions of the encircling mountains. Sky Walker was satisfied with the location, even though it would take more lookouts to preserve their safety. There were trees in the valley for shade, a mountain water supply from several streams, and the higher elevation provided a cooler climate.

The mountains led into the Verde Barranca, which stretched to the Pacific Ocean and contained numerous farms, villages, and towns. There were also various routes through the mountains that the Apaches could follow in order to strike in other valleys. A Mexican army unit was stationed at Carbo, ten miles from Sky Walker's mountain hideout. But the soldiers would not be able to penetrate the stronghold without being ambushed.

For two nights, Sky Walker and his braves scouted the village of Santa Clara, which was closest to the Sierra Madres. The small farming community contained only two dozen houses and a grain storage building. Just before sunrise on the fourth day, the Apaches struck.

The entire village was suddenly turned into a screaming, burning town. The farmers were put to death, but the majority of the women and children were kept alive to be used as slaves by the Apache band. Sky Walker's group was well stocked with supplies as they moved quickly back into the mountains.

"It has been a good day for us," Sitting Bear told Sky Walker. "We have captured many women and children to help with the work. Our families will be proud."

"Yes. It went well," Sky Walker admitted.

But the Apache leader was puzzled. Why were the villages so unprotected? So easily attacked?

***

The Apache chief would soon find out that Santa Clara was on a huge land grant that had been given to Constantine Vorshoff. The Russian army officer, now turned Mexican general, was in charge of military operations in Sonora and Chihuahua, the two northernmost Mexican states. Within twenty-four hours, Vorshoff and a hundred of his Mexican cavalry would be headed towards the scene of the massacre. Even the Mexican banditos feared Vorshoff's wrath and steered clear of the towns on his private land holdings.

***

"Look at that one," Sitting Bear said, pointing to a stout Mexican woman who marched along with her back straight and a look of determination in her eyes. "It'll take a lot of beatings to get her to be a good slave. But she is a strong one."

Sky Walker and Sitting Bear sat on their horses looking at the captives march into the mountains. The woman to whom Sitting Bear had referred just happened to be visiting friends in the village on the day of the attack. Her name was Anna Bustamante.

***

The Montoya brothers, accompanied by ten of the Bustamante vaqueros, arrived at the nearby village of Castillo three days later. Don Carlos had implored Ricardo to attempt to find and free his sister. Ricardo had agreed to do what he could. Now he was seeking out Mexicans who had lived in or near the mountains. He needed background information on this section of the Sierra Madre Range, and probable locations where the Indians might have established a camp.

The mayor of Castillo brought forth several men who were familiar with the surrounding mountains. Little by little, the Montoyas pieced together a map of the area, along with suggested reconnaissance routes. The mountains were tall, jagged, and impassable in many locations. Long valleys cut through and around other peaks. At the base of the mountains was the desert. The higher valleys were lush and green, and at the extreme altitudes the slopes were covered with forests of pine and aspen.

One old miner in particular, Pepe Flores, impressed Ricardo with his slow but precise description of the area. Flores had mined the surrounding mountains for fifty years and knew every crevice and crag. He marked off several diagrammed routes that Ricardo could take to investigate them.

Rafael had accompanied Ricardo on the mission. "I have nothing better to do at the moment," he had told Ricardo.

The brothers entered the mountains at the point where the Apaches had taken their captives. But less than a quarter of a mile later they had lost the trail because of the rocky terrain. The band could have taken a dozen different paths in and around various piles of boulders and rocky crags. The brothers were able to follow the map easily, but the going was slow and tedious.

Often they could not use their horses and had the wearisome task of climbing on foot until they could look down and scan the surrounding area with binoculars. A day and a half passed before they located the Indian camp. From a northern mountaintop, Ricardo looked south into a long valley surrounded by other peaks. The main entrance was from the west, and there were smaller exits to the south and east.

"They must have eight or ten women and a dozen children as captives," Rafael said as he studied the camp through the binoculars. "There's not more than two dozen braves of fighting age."

Rafael lay on his stomach with his weight on his elbows. He pulled the binoculars down from his eyes and rolled over on his back. Ricardo was lying beside him.

"I haven't been able to pick out the sentries," said Rafael.

Ricardo rolled over and pointed to an eastern peak above the other mountaintops. "There's probably one up there, and maybe one down at the southern end," he said.

"I agree," said Rafael. "It will be difficult to surprise them."

The brothers rested and then began their slow descent out of the mountains.

***

It was near dusk on the second night before they returned to Castillo. The mayor met them.

"General Vorshoff is back and awaits you at his hacienda, two miles to the west," said the mayor.

Ricardo turned to his brother. "Let's go there now, Rafael. I want to meet this man I've heard so much about."

Fifteen minutes later, they were at the general's hacienda.

The main ranch house was surrounded by tall trees. At the rear, there were long rows of barracks constructed to house Vorshoff's soldiers when it was necessary that they be with him. He was a military man first and a rancher second.

Guards admitted the two men through the gates into the courtyard. They dismounted and walked up the front steps. Another soldier opened the door for them, and they gave their names and waited to be announced. The Montoyas were quickly ushered into a long room that once had been the formal dining hall. Now, maps covered the walls, and a large conference table stood in the center of the room. Standing next to the table was a tall man dressed in a light brown army uniform. His arms were crossed behind his back.

General Vorshoff was an impressive man. He was as tall as Ricardo, powerfully built, and carried himself with dignity and pride. Vorshoff had extremely large gray eyes, radiating intelligence and sensitivity. He had long, gray-black hair and a dramatic mustache that stretched downward and then curled up at the ends, adding a striking touch to the picture of Mexico's legendary Indian fighter.

Ricardo and Rafael advanced and introduced themselves to Vorshoff.

"I have heard much about you, Mr. Montoya," said the general in a deep baritone voice directed toward Ricardo.

"Not as much as I've heard about you," said Ricardo.

The three men sat down, and servants hastened to bring them refreshments.

Vorshoff's large eyes fastened on Ricardo. "Word of your recent exploits against the Apaches has come back to me. Your plans were excellent, they were carried out efficiently, and you were highly successful. These are the things by which a man is measured."

Ricardo smiled. "Thank you."

"Being a military man, I have many sources of information. Some people I must seek out. Others try to impress me by keeping me informed. And, others sell me information. Seldom have I received reports on a man's activities such as I have received about you," said Vorshoff. "The people of Sonora are beginning to look upon you as some type of folk hero."

Rafael grinned. "Don't believe everything you hear, General."

The men laughed.

"Here is a letter from Don Carlos Bustamante," said Ricardo, and handed the correspondence to Vorshoff.

The general read the note, and his gray eyes settled again on Ricardo.

"Don Carlos and I have been friends for many years. I am sorry to hear that his sister is one of the captives. Indian raids this far west are rare," said Vorshoff. "What can you tell me of this band?"

"The group is led by a Chiricahua named Sky Walker. His band escaped from the San Carlos Indian Reservation. He is a wise, intelligent leader," said Ricardo. "It surprised me that we were able to trap so many of his braves at the head of the Sierra Madres."

"Even the best military minds make mistakes," commented Vorshoff.

Rafael and Ricardo took turns explaining the details about Sky Walker's camp and the logistics of invading it. They walked over to a large wall map, and Vorshoff pointed out the valley.

"The topography may not be exactly what you have seen. These maps were pieced together with information obtained from many sources," said the general.

Ricardo studied the area for a moment. "It's close enough. Here is the main entrance to the valley." And he traced it with his finger.

"How would you suggest that we advance?" Vorshoff asked.

"My brother and I discussed a plan of attack when we were coming here. In fact, Rafael had the idea originally," said Ricardo.

Vorshoff looked at Rafael. "Two brothers with military minds?" he asked, smiling.

Rafael diagrammed what he had in mind, and Ricardo added to it. Vorshoff listened intently, closely studied the map, and nodded his head in agreement.

"Yes," he murmured. "It's a good plan of attack. I might suggest that other detachments of my troops be positioned here and here to cut off escape routes." He pointed to additional locations.

"Much will depend on how quickly and successfully we can move men into the main attack positions," Ricardo noted. "There's no telling how long they will stay in that area."

Vorshoff continued to study the wall map and then turned to Ricardo. "I will want you and your brother to direct my men from the main attack position here," he said as he pointed to the map. "Will you do me the honor?"

"It is you who honor us," Ricardo said, and smiled.

The men now discussed the coming campaign in detail. It was decided that they would depart the following morning.

Their conversation was interrupted when a group of horsemen rode up outside. An obviously distraught servant hurried into the room and whispered something in Vorshoff's ear.

"Tell him I'll be with him in a moment," said Vorshoff. Then he turned to the Montoya brothers. "Gentlemen, it seems we have a visitor. Don Diego Salazar is here with a number of his vaqueros."

Ricardo and Rafael looked at each other in surprise.

"There are some things you should know, General," said Ricardo.

"I have heard rumors. I would like to hear from you before I ask Don Diego to come in," said Vorshoff.

Ricardo and Rafael provided Vorshoff with a brief history of their relationship with Salazar, how each had been dismissed, and how Ricardo had rescued Rafael.

"Why do you think you fell from favor?" Vorshoff asked Ricardo.

Ricardo glanced at his brother. "Rafael tells me that Don Diego began to feel threatened by me. He said I began making decisions on my own and did not give Salazar enough...praise."

Vorshoff's eyes studied Ricardo. Then he looked a Rafael. "How could you continue to work for a man who had a reward offered for your brother?"

Rafael looked uncomfortable. "When I learned of information concerning my brother's safety, I passed it on to Ricardo. However, I always carried out my job to the best of my ability. Don Diego's safety was never in question."

"And, the reason you are here is because of your friendship for Don Carlos Bustamante?" Vorshoff asked.

Rafael smiled. "Rather, Ricardo's close friendship with his daughter."

Ricardo looked embarrassed and gave his brother a sharp look. A slight smile passed over Vorshoff's lips. He motioned for one of the servants to come forward.

"Show Don Diego in," the general said.

Salazar almost ran into the room. "General, it is my pleasure to see you again," he said loudly.

"Don Diego, it is good to see you, too," said Vorshoff.

There was more than a foot difference in the height of the men, making Salazar appear more puny than ever. His eyes flickered toward the brothers and then back to General Vorshoff.

"These men are wanted for crimes they committed against me and my property," Don Diego said in a haughty voice.

"Wanted by whom?" the general asked calmly.

A look of surprise came over Don Diego's face. "Wanted by me, of course. They have stolen horses from my rancho, money from my house, and even attacked me personally."

"Those charges are not true," Ricardo said in an even voice.

A look of hatred passed over Salazar's face, and he looked back at Vorshoff. "I would ask that you turn them over to me. I shall see that justice is done."

"These men are my guests," said Vorshoff. "Whatever differences you have had, it is none of my concern."

"Would you protect criminals?" Salazar cried out.

Vorshoff's eyes blazed and he stepped forward and looked down at Don Diego. "I have heard enough of this foolishness. I am the military commander of this state. More than one man has been clapped in irons for the insolence you have displayed. Now state your business!" he bellowed.

Salazar's eyes blinked several times under the onslaught, and he appeared to physically shrink away from the general. He suddenly looked frightened and took a step backward. "I meant nothing of the sort, General. I assure you, I have only the highest respect and honor for you. I am sorry if you took offense to what I said. I withdraw the statement. I'm here only to help," Don Diego repeated nervously.

"What do you mean?" asked the general.

"I heard about the Apaches capturing the sister of Don Carlos Bustamante. I came with some of my men to see if we could be of assistance. We must help one another," said Don Diego.

Vorshoff strolled over to a large chair and sat down. He motioned for the other men to take seats. Salazar was obviously petrified, and his body twitched. Ricardo gave Rafael a skeptical look.

"It was my understanding that you and Don Carlos were enemies," said Vorshoff.

Salazar looked surprised. "Any differences we once had are a thing of the past. My main thought is only to help him."

Vorshoff nodded his head in agreement. As a military commander, one of his primary goals was to get the land barons to work together for common causes and defense. The ranchers of northern Mexico were the backbone of the country's political and social integrity. Their solidarity, singleness of purpose, and cooperation were the key ingredients to a successful government.

The general's huge eyes bore into Salazar, but his thoughts were unreadable. "We are leaving at daybreak. You are welcome to join us," he said. "Your men will be billeted in back. Raul will show you to your room here in the house." He motioned to one of the servants.

From his expression, it was obvious that Don Diego did not like being dismissed. He stood up, said good evening to the general, and left.

"What are you thinking?" Vorshoff asked the two brothers.

"Don Carlos Bustamante would never become friends with a man who tried to kill him. That is certain," said Ricardo.

"Then why is he here?" the general asked.

"I know why," said Rafael. "He hates Ricardo to the point that he will go to any length to kill him. Someone on Don Carlos's hacienda is supplying Don Diego with information, probably for a heavy price. When Don Diego learned that Ricardo would come south to help find the Apaches, he brought men to kill him. I'm sure he intends that Ricardo shall never leave the mountains alive. There are many opportunities during a battle to shoot a man on your own side."

"I find it hard to believe that any man could be so consumed with hatred for another," said Vorshoff.

Rafael leaned forward and placed his arms on the table. "I'd be willing to wager that the men with Don Diego are not vaqueros but hired gunmen. There are few men on the ranch who dislike Ricardo enough to hunt him down and kill him."

Vorshoff looked at Ricardo. "What do you think?"

"I agree with my brother. Don Diego does whatever he wants to do, regardless of whether it is right or wrong," said Ricardo.

***

At dawn, the men assembled in the courtyard. Nearly one hundred of Vorshoff's cavalry and ten of Bustamante's vaqueros were ready to ride. Vorshoff and Salazar emerged from the ranch house and stood at the head of the steps. The troops and cowboys faced them, awaiting orders. Salazar suddenly realized that his men were not present.

"Where are my men? They're supposed to be here," said Don Diego. His head turned anxiously from side to side.

Vorshoff looked down at the rancher and said coolly, "They have been detained."

"Why?" asked Salazar in a frantic voice.

"It was discovered, upon interrogation, that two of your riders are wanted for murder in the City of Chihuahua. They will all be detained until thorough investigations are made concerning their backgrounds," Vorshoff said resolutely.

Salazar's eyes were wide with fear. Sweat formed on his brow. "I must protest...."

Vorshoff's large gray eyes studied Salazar intently. "Where did you get those men? They certainly aren't vaqueros."

Salazar's composure began to crumble in front of the assembled horsemen. "I...I hired them because they were good fighters. I...I didn't know they were criminals," he pleaded.

The general put on his gloves and glanced at Don Diego. "Well, never mind. You'll still get your chance to help Don Carlos. You may ride with the Bustamante vaqueros."

Salazar suddenly choked and began coughing and gasping for breath. "No!" he croaked.

"Are you all right?" asked the general.

"Yes," said Salazar. "I mean, no! I mean, I don't want to be with the Montoyas. They are my enemies."

Vorshoff had had enough of Salazar. "You will stay with the Bustamante riders," the general stated in his deep voice. "You said Don Carlos is a friend of yours, and that's why you're here. Now, prove it."

CHAPTER 15

The military column moved across the prairie and into the mountains in the early morning. Wagons loaded with food, tents, ammunition, and other supplies accompanied the long line of cavalry. Ricardo and Rafael rode at the head of the column with General Vorshoff. Bustamante's vaqueros were at the rear along with Don Diego. Dust from the horses was always worst for the rear guard, and Salazar's beautiful black clothing was soon covered with a layer of tan dust.

At noon, the troops were split into four groups, each of which took a different trail toward their various destinations. Salazar and the vaqueros stayed with General Vorshoff. This group would be the central force most likely to meet the Indians if they made a break out of the mountains.

Don Diego looked miserable. He had no protective forces of his own. The rancher was hot, tired, and covered with dirt. Vorshoff all but ignored Salazar as he conferred with his officers, reviewed maps, checked equipment, and surveyed the mountains with his binoculars.

By nightfall, Vorshoff was satisfied that everything was proceeding as planned, and he became more cordial, inviting Salazar to have dinner at his campfire. Ricardo and Rafael had left with one of the smaller groups of soldiers early in the day. Some of Don Diego's courage was returning.

The general and Salazar talked about cattle, the burgeoning market in Arizona, and Mexican politics.

"I intend to seek appointment as governor of Sonora," Salazar told Vorshoff. "I have the largest land holdings in the state and should be entitled to such a position now that Canandra is stepping down."

Vorshoff tried to hold back a smile. Salazar was not well thought of by his peers, the military, or the officials in the Mexican government. Vorshoff had to deal with the governor, Miguel Canandra, on a weekly basis, and was aware of how important it was to have a man of stature in that position.

The fool wants me to support him, thought Vorshoff. He thought for a moment and then asked, "The other ranchers would have to support you. Can you get their support?"

"No problem," said Don Diego. "They all know me quite well."

"I'm sure that's true," said the general.

Salazar didn't know whether the statement had a double meaning or not. He decided to continue. "Your recommendation will be most important," he said. "The government listens closely to you."

Vorshoff took a sip of hot coffee. His giant hand enveloped the cup. "It is true that they listen to me."

"I would be very grateful if I could get your backing," Don Diego said quietly.

Salazar's eyes were mere slits as he appraised the general.

"At the moment, I'm not prepared to support any one person. I am looking at a number of prospective candidates," Vorshoff said.

Salazar looked like a cunning weasel as he dangled his bait. "Your range is short of beef. I would be prepared to offer you ten thousand head of cattle in exchange for your backing."

Vorshoff coldly appraised the rancher. He saw before him a small, evil man who firmly believed every person had a price. The thought that offering a bribe might offend a man's dignity or code of ethics never entered Salazar's mind.

"One of the reasons the government has empowered me with this command is that I do not take bribes," Vorshoff said in his deep voice.

Salazar shrugged his shoulders. "Consider it a loan."

The general tried to hold back his anger. "I wouldn't back you under any circumstance. The type of man I intend to recommend will be honest. He will have a reputation for fairness in his dealings, compassion for his fellow man, and above all, a code of ethics that is unquestionable. You fail miserably in all areas. Salazar's eyes were wide, and his mouth opened slightly in disbelief. "Surely you mistake what I said," Don Diego blurted out.

Vorshoff rose from the ground and dusted himself off. He looked steadily at Salazar. "There's no mistaking what you say or what you are. Everything I've heard about you is true, and none of it is good."

The general walked off and left the small rancher in a momentary state of shock.

***

Ricardo, Rafael, and their party of soldiers had made their way south and then east around the mountains, encircling Sky Walker's camp. By nightfall they had moved slowly up the rocky cliffs to a point where they had to leave the horses and begin climbing. Progress was slow, and at times they would have to wait while one soldier would climb up thirty or forty feet and lower a rope so they could follow.

The men had to traverse sideways whenever they encountered a sheer cliff. The moon was full and the stars shone brightly, but progress was still extremely slow. It was nearly four in the morning by the time they reached their destination, a jagged mountaintop that resembled the top of a dinosaur's back. The soldiers spread out and climbed down behind boulders and into crevices to wait for the morning's first light.

The other two elements of the cavalry unit had proceeded north and southeast to cut off other escape routes that Ricardo and Vorshoff had anticipated.

As the first streaks of sunlight came over the horizon, Ricardo used binoculars to check out the most likely positions where lookouts would be stationed. He was unable to spot them.

Wickiups were spread throughout the grassy mountain meadow. Streams had been dammed in two areas to provide drinking water for the animals. Squaws were just beginning to start the morning fires. Ricardo judged that the shooting range would be six hundred to seven hundred feet.

"It's time, Rafael," said Ricardo. "The soldiers are bunched too closely together. It doesn't matter if we're seen now. Take ten men and spread them along the mountain's ridge to the left. I'll do the same to the right."

The men followed the two Montoya brothers, and the line began to spread. Suddenly, an Indian sentry spotted the soldiers and shouted down into the canyon. The women stopped what they were doing and shaded their eyes. The sun was just coming over the mountain peak behind the soldiers when the first shot was fired.

One of the Indian scouts steadied his rifle and shot a soldier through the front of his tan uniform. He fell on top of a large boulder, and his hat sailed off into space.

"Get him," Rafael yelled.

A volley of shots rang out, and the rocks exploded in splinters around the Indian's head and shoulders. One of the twenty-five slugs found its mark and he slumped out of sight.

The valley suddenly came to life with a crescendo of cries and screams from the Indian women. The soldiers began firing, and several squaws went down. Braves burst out of the wickiups and ran for shelter behind boulders or small trees.

"Shoot at the men!" Ricardo shouted. "Save your bullets for the men!"

The scene was one of mass confusion as bullets rained down on the encampment. Indians were running in every direction like ants coming out of the ground.

Another sentry began firing at the troopers. He was well hidden in a rock crevice, and Ricardo fired four shots before he finally wounded the Apache.

The horses broke loose from the corral and began galloping back and forth in the canyon, adding even more confusion to the scene. The death toll began to mount as more and more of the band went down before the relentless gunfire of the Mexican soldiers.

Sky Walker stayed inside his wickiup with his wife and two sons until he could seize an opportunity to escape. A bridled horse galloped past the wickiup's opening and the chief jumped out and grabbed it around the neck. The horse reared and whinnied, but Sky Walker held fast to its reins. He leaped onto the horse's back and stayed low as it continued to gallop back and forth with the other confused animals.

Sky Walker came alongside a reddish-brown stallion and leaped from his horse to the back of the stallion, but he kept the reins of the first horse in his hand and pulled both horses to a stop in front of his wickiup. His wife was up behind him in a flash, and his two sons clambered up on the other horse.

They rode toward the main entrance to the canyon. Several other braves had also mounted animals and fled after their chief.

"Shoot the ones on the horses!" Rafael yelled. "Shoot the bucks off the horses!"

The rifle blasts echoed back and forth off the canyon walls. Apaches continued to run in a helter-skelter manner, and the horses obscured the aim of the soldiers. More and more of the Indians began to run toward the three main canyon exits.

As soon as Sky Walker went around a bend in the canyon wall and was out of sight of the attackers, he pulled his horse up. In the space of a few moments, seven other braves joined him. When it became apparent that no other warriors were coming, Sky Walker signaled his men and they rode into the foothills. He veered to the right and into a small gorge following the edge of the main canyon as it emptied out into the hills that led down to the flat country. Sky Walker's decision to follow the narrow ravine along the edge of the canyon took his band out of view of the main body of attackers lying in wait.

***

Vorshoff and his soldiers, Salazar, and the Bustamante vaqueros were all spread across the canyon mouth awaiting the exodus. They were behind rocks, in gullies, and lying behind rises in the ground. Don Diego Salazar was in the small ravine sitting behind a boulder. He had thought this would put him on the edge of the fighting and keep him out of the conflict. He was sweating profusely, and wiped the perspiration from his mustache and beard.

Sky Walker and his party swept down the gulley. Salazar looked up in disbelief as the Indians galloped toward him. He stood up to run, but was frozen in his tracks. He had his revolver in his hand, but fear made him forget he had a weapon.

Sky Walker had grabbed his war lance as he rode away from the wickiup and still held the battle symbol in his right hand. As he reached Don Diego, he drove the spear through Salazar's stomach. The rancher screamed and dropped to the ground, twisting and turning in agony. Don Diego looked like a black bug impaled on the end of a pin, squirming and writhing as he tried to get free. The Apaches' horses rode over Salazar, throwing his body about like a rag doll. In a flash, they were by him and out into the open.

Vorshoff and his soldiers came running toward the gorge and began firing at the Apaches as they disappeared into another ravine. Two of the Apaches were hit and went down.

Another group of Indians, comprised mostly of squaws and older boys, now reached the head of the canyon. Some were on horses, while others were running. They had few weapons and concentrated on escape rather than fighting the enemy. Vorshoff's soldiers and the vaqueros directed heavy fire at them. Guns flashed everywhere, and a dust cloud rose to obliterate vision. Yells from the soldiers and screams from the women and children turned the scene to one of total pandemonium.

***

Sky Walker halted his braves when they had left the gunfire well behind. "Stay here," he told his wife and sons.

He motioned with his arm and the braves followed him back the way they had come. They reached the mouth of the canyon, dismounted, and took defensive positions behind rocks. One brave held all the horses. Sky Walker and the other four Apaches directed their fire at the soldiers and vaqueros, who had their backs to the Indians.

***

Vorshoff was wounded in the right arm and shifted his revolver to his left hand. "Turn and fire at them!" he yelled. He pointed at Sky Walker and his braves, who had taken cover.

The soldiers and cowboys began running for the sides of the canyon, where the rocks and boulders were larger and afforded more protection. The squaws and older Indian boys raced through the battlefield past Sky Walker and the defenders. But their number had been greatly reduced. Of the two dozen who reached the battle area, only seven survived.

Three braves thundered down the ravine where Sky Walker had made his escape, and ran headlong into six troopers. The men fired at each other at point-blank range. Horses reared, and two braves were knocked from their animals. One of them jumped into the midst of the soldiers, slashing at the troopers with his knife. He was riddled with bullets, but thrust his knife into a soldier's stomach before he died. The third Apache urged his horse forward and rode over the Mexican troopers. They were knocked right and left as his mount thundered forward.

The men in Sky Walker's last wall of defense were firing mercilessly on the soldiers.

"Get under cover!" Vorshoff roared to his men.

A bullet grazed his right leg before the general leaped behind some rocks. After this battle was over, he would have two more scars to add to his array of war injuries.

When no other Apaches exited the valley, Sky Walker and his men mounted up and rode after the disappearing squaws and children.

Vorshoff hobbled out from behind his rock and gave orders to his captain. "Get as many men together as you can. Ride after them as a formation. If they stay in the flats, you should be able to catch them. If they head back into the mountains, don't get ambushed!"

The troopers' horses had been scattered during the battle, and men were running after them, trying to mount so they could give chase. A group of twenty soldiers finally rounded up mounts and thundered after the remnants of the Apache band.

***

Sky Walker immediately headed back into another valley, which wound its way upward into the Sierra Madres. When he reached the ambush site he was looking for, the chief deployed his men on both sides of the narrow canyon walls. The women and children continued on their flight to safety.

The soldiers were in hot pursuit, with only one objective driving them: Engage the enemy. The six remaining braves fired one volley into the front ranks of the troopers. Soldiers and horses fell in every direction. The momentum of the horsemen behind the front ranks created a plug, and the troopers were momentarily helpless. The Indians continued to fire one round after another, and only the soldiers at the rear of the formation were able to turn their mounts and ride for freedom. Fifteen of the pursuing soldiers were killed or wounded.

The chief again ordered his men down out of the rocks and they quickly finished off the wounded troopers. They took the newer rifles and ammunition, plus any food the dead soldiers had on them, and continued their flight.

***

Within minutes after the battle had begun in the huge meadow, another segment of the Apache band had fled to the far northern end of the canyon. Five warriors and more than three dozen women and children made it into the foothills.

These Indians did not take the path anticipated by the detachment of soldiers who had been deployed to stop them. The braves climbed to a higher altitude and made the women and children follow them. They intended to climb high into the mountains and make their pursuers follow them on foot. But the Indians were in plain sight while they climbed the first thirty feet, and the soldiers sent volley after volley into their ranks.

Like raindrops, the bodies of the women and children fell from the canyon wall. Only fifteen squaws, children, and braves made it into the sanctuary of the higher elevations, where the soldiers' firing line was obscured by rock formations.

After climbing for several hundred feet, the braves reached a plateau. They lay down on their stomachs and waited for the soldiers. The Apaches let loose their fire only when the soldiers were just below them. The first round of firing killed three troopers and wounded two others. Vorshoff's men threw themselves backward and slid or rolled down behind rock outcroppings.

A young lieutenant, Jose Vasquez, ordered his troops to skirt the defensive position held by the Indians and climb to a higher elevation along another section of the mountain. The Indians could hear the rocks falling as the troops made their climb, and they also began climbing.

The two forces came together on a level section that was pockmarked with small craters, rock ridges, and a red rock arch that created a natural bridge forty feet high.

The Indians arrived first and poured a hail of bullets into the soldiers. But the return fire from the troopers killed two of the remaining warriors. Young Indian boys grabbed their fathers' rifles and continued to fire until they fell. Squaws picked up whatever weapons they could find and fired at the advancing soldiers. They were mowed down like wheat.

More than a dozen soldiers advanced onto the plateau. They moved from one body to another and finished them off if they were still alive. A Mexican rolled one warrior over, and the buck used his revolver to shoot the trooper through the forehead. Three other soldiers fired simultaneously at the dying Apache.

***

The third group of Apaches was made up entirely of women and children, and they attempted to escape through a mountain passage to the southeast. They ran headlong into Vorshoff's third contingent of troops and fled back the way they had come.

Ricardo and the other attackers who had surprised the Apache camp climbed down and advanced on the wickiups that were still standing.

"Cease firing!" Ricardo yelled. "Don't shoot anyone else unless you're fired upon."

The remnants of the third group came running back toward the wickiups, and a soldier standing next to Ricardo raised his rifle to shoot the woman in front. Ricardo slapped his rifle barrel downward.

"I said there'll be no more shooting, and I meant it!" he roared. "Round up the remainder of them and put them in that corral," he said, pointing to a small enclosure up against a rock wall.

Cautiously, the troops explored the wickiups one after another. Some women and children were found hiding and were promptly pulled out and herded into the corral.

About fifty yards in front of him, Ricardo could see a heavyset woman chasing a squaw with a switch. The big woman was moving at a rapid pace to keep up with the young squaw, who was dodging and darting in and out among the rocks.

Ricardo just shook his head. He had found Aunt Anna alive and in her usual frame of mind. Ricardo caught up with her and took her by the arm. She jerked it away and stared at Montoya in disbelief.

"You!" she said. "What are you doing here?"

"Don Carlos sent me to find you."

She fixed him with one of her ice-melting gazes. "If you think this changes my opinion of you, you're wrong. Maria's emotions should not be trifled with."

Ricardo's mouth dropped open. "I...," he began, but stopped, speechless. He turned quickly and walked away.

He forgot about her a moment later when a wounded General Vorshoff and his soldiers came riding into the valley. Ricardo helped him dismount.

"How bad are the wounds?" Ricardo asked.

Vorshoff snorted. "I've had worse."

"We haven't located the chief, Sky Walker."

The general looked around the clearing. He turned to one of his aides.

"Gather every piece of equipment and food the Apaches have and burn them," he ordered. "Burn the wickiups, too." Vorshoff turned back to Montoya. "In answer to your statement, my men had the pleasure of encountering Sky Walker and some of his braves. That Indian is the best fighter I've ever seen. He and three or four of his braves and a few women and children escaped." The old soldier shook his head. "They killed twenty of my soldiers. Fifteen of them died when they were caught in a ravine as they were pursuing the Apaches."

Ricardo shook his head in sympathy. "Where's Salazar?"

"He's dead, too," said the weary general. "I can't say that I'm sorry."

"What?" Ricardo said in amazement.

"Salazar was speared through the stomach. He bled to death."

"Dead! I can't believe he's dead," said Ricardo. He suddenly felt a weight lifting from his shoulders.

Rafael came running up to his brother. "Did you hear the news?"

"Yes," said Ricardo, still shocked by the fact that his hated adversary was no more.

"It means freedom for us to travel and do whatever we wish," said Rafael.

The Montoyas supervised the rounding up of the remainder of Sky Walker's band. Of the more than one hundred women and children, only sixteen were left alive. No warriors had survived except for those few with Sky Walker.

The soldiers set fire to everything that would burn. The beautiful green valley was filled with smoke as the procession—soldiers, cowboys, and their captives—began the march out of the mountains. Most of the Mexican women and children had been rescued alive and unharmed. The Mexican government would credit General Vorshoff with another brilliant victory and award him additional medals.

***

Sky Walker and the few survivors from his band viewed the procession silently. They were gathered among the rocks on the mountainside overlooking the plains that stretched to the Sea of Cortez.

The chief turned his head and surveyed what few followers still remained alive. *There will be no problem obtaining food now*, he thought. The wind blew strong, and he suddenly felt cold and lonely in the wilderness.

CHAPTER 16

Harry Palmer ushered Victoria Barringer into his office and over to the couch he used for special visitors.

"Victoria, you look more lovely each time I see you," said the gray-haired attorney.

The matriarch smiled her most dazzling smile. She was decked out as impeccably as ever. "One of the things I've always liked about you, Harry, is your ability to lie so convincingly," she said, and her eyes sparkled.

Victoria settled on the couch with a grace and elegance that never ceased to amaze Palmer. When both had been younger, Palmer had had it in his mind to marry Victoria after her husband died. However, the head of the Barringer empire had decided that she wished to rule alone. So, Harry confined his activities to ironing out all legal entanglements that the Barringer juggernaut blundered into.

Palmer's dark blue eyes were intelligent and analytical. Coupled with his distinguished good looks, his pragmatic approach to solving problems had built him a highly successful practice.

"You do me great honor I think, madam," said Palmer in a good-natured voice.

Victoria's piercing eyes contemplated Palmer. Her fingers gently tapped the arm of the couch, and she cocked her head to one side. "Maybe I should have accepted your proposal twenty years ago, Harry," she said in a sly manner.

The smile left Palmer's face for an instant. "I think you're playing a game," said the lawyer. "I was serious, you know."

"It might have been easier if you had run the ranch," she said.

Harry grinned. "But not nearly as much fun for you."

Victoria laughed melodically. "Oh, Harry, I do enjoy being with you. But I'm not one to share. I fear our strong wills and personalities would have clashed," she said in a sincere voice.

Palmer shrugged his shoulders. "Perhaps you're right. I would have taken the chance, though."

They discussed ranch business for the next half hour. Palmer had coffee served in his office, and he looked up to see Victoria's eyes inspecting him over the top of her cup as she drank.

"You have another roundup coming up soon," said Palmer. "I have a couple of new suggestions for investments that could bring immense dividends. You know you can't spend all the money you make from cattle...." Palmer stopped because he sensed that her mind was elsewhere. "Are you bothering to listen to me?" he asked.

"Of course I am, Harry. But I have some other news for you. James is coming back to the ranch," she said, and riveted her eyes on the attorney.

Palmer raised his eyebrows. "It means more trouble."

"That's why I'm here."

"I don't know what I can do. John has it in his mind that James is some type of threat to him. I think he may try to eliminate him again," Palmer said in a steady voice.

Victoria put her coffee cup down and sat back on the couch.

"Your power of observation is every bit as acute as in past years," said Victoria. "I intend to see that such a confrontation does not transpire."

"How?"

Victoria smiled, and her expression was that of a sly cat. "By changing my will to read that if James is killed, John is automatically written out of any inheritance."

Palmer exhaled deeply. "That's pretty severe."

She dropped the subtle tone of her previous conversation. "I need men. I need heirs. I don't want them killing each other off. It's as simple as that."

Harry scratched his head and looked somewhat skeptical. Then he looked at the proud woman and decided to be straightforward. "After you're gone, John just might succeed. Don't you think you're putting off the inevitable?"

Victoria smiled, once again the schemer. "I intend to live a long, long time. Besides, this land is becoming more civilized every year. In years to come, law and order will be the norm. And don't forget William. He'll be married and raising a family before long."

"William?" Palmer said in a surprised voice.

"Yes. He's quite capable, you know. He doesn't know it yet, but he's going to marry Agatha Hale," Victoria said with a note of triumph in her voice.

Palmer just shook his head. "You never cease to amaze me, Victoria. If you'd been born a man, I think you'd have been president."

"Maybe, although the job is confining," she said matter-of-factly.

They both laughed. Palmer quickly drew up the codicil to the will, had it properly witnessed, and sent it over to be filed in the courthouse.

The lawyer walked with Victoria to her stylish carriage. "When do you intend to tell him?" he said, referring to John Barringer.

"Tonight at dinner. I haven't decided whether I'll wait until dessert or let him know as the entrée is being served."

Palmer smiled and watched the carriage pull away. *She'd have been too much for me to handle*, he thought.

**

Ricardo and the Indian women and children, accompanied by Bustamante vaqueros, began the long ride through the Nogales Pass on their way to the border. The peons turned out by the dozens to watch. Both sides of the hard-packed dirt road were lined with Mexicans, who began cheering when they recognized Ricardo.

"Your reputation precedes you, Brother," Rafael said, smiling.

Ricardo felt embarrassed by the tribute.

"They think you're some kind of a hero," said Rafael. "They don't know you like I do."

The procession wound its way through the narrow Nogales city streets. Crowds gathered to view the hated enemy. But the lowly squaws and children were hunched over their horses with their heads down. It was disgraceful to them to be paraded like animals before the Mexicans. All of them had lost husbands or fathers in the fighting, and knew they were heading back to captivity.

On the American side of the border, they stopped and camped. Vorshoff had sent messengers to the U.S. Army forts, informing them of the battle and indicating that the captives would be brought to Nogales for transfer to American

196

authority. The cavalry had not yet arrived. The sixteen Indians were fed and allowed to relax in the shade of a stand of walnut trees.

In the distance, Ricardo could see a cloud of dust. As the riders came closer, it became evident that the men were not cavalry.

"Rafael. Get the Indians in among the trees. See that the men take cover. Do nothing unless I give the word," Ricardo ordered.

The Indians were herded in among the walnut trees, and the Bustamante vaqueros took cover there as well. Ricardo waited on his palomino. He was dressed in his usual tan vaquero's outfit, and his eyes were hard and his jaw set. Montoya was in no mood for the threat he knew was coming.

The band of horsemen drew up in front of Ricardo. Most were miners dressed in an assortment of dirty clothing and floppy hats.

"What do you want?" Ricardo stated in a level voice.

The miners looked at one another and then at the Apaches they could glimpse among the trees. A fat man with pig-like eyes pointed at the Indians. "We want them. They's part of the band that done killed some of our friends. The dirty, thievin' murderers!"

Ricardo inspected the group and noted that most of the men were drunk. He made his decision. "These Indians are to be turned over to the U.S. Calvary," he said firmly.

The fat miner spat a stream of tobacco, and part of it ran down the front of his dirty blue shirt. "We ain't leavin' without 'em. Stand aside or we'll string you up with those devils."

Ricardo walked his horse forward until he was abreast of the miner.

"There's nothing but women and children left. Look at them!" Ricardo ordered. "They're harmless, and they're going back to live like animals. Is that what you're going to die for?"

The fat man looked suspiciously at Ricardo. "What do you mean, die?"

Montoya's eyes bore into the miner. "You're the leader, which means I'll shoot you as soon as the first man raises his rifle."

The big miner's mouth opened slightly, revealing rotten, tobacco-stained teeth. "I ain't no leader," he said. Sweat popped out on his forehead.

Montoya had his rifle across his saddle. He raised the weapon and struck the miner across the forehead with a quick blow. The man's eyes rolled back in his head and he pitched backward off his horse. He hit the ground with a thud and lay still.

"Pick him up and put him over his horse," Montoya ordered.

Courage left the small band of miners. Two men dismounted and helped lift the fat man and throw him over his horse. They tied him down and then remounted.

"Weren't no cause to do that," one miner said quietly.

"Move out!" Ricardo ordered in a hard voice.

The group turned their horses and headed back the way they had come. Rafael walked out from the trees and joined Ricardo.

"I hope those soldiers get here soon. There's a girl waiting for me in Hermosillo," Rafael said, and grinned.

Ricardo smiled teasingly. "Don't worry. Someone's probably looking after her."

Two hours later the soldiers rode up. Lieutenant Fredericks was at the head of the column, sporting new captain's bars on his shoulder. Ricardo introduced the cavalry officer to his brother.

"Is this all of them?" Fredericks asked.

"Their chief, Sky Walker, and perhaps ten others are still in Mexico. Half of those are women and children," said Ricardo.

As they were being herded together for the trip back to the reservation, Fredericks stared at the wailing and depressed women and children.

"What a terrible ending. They'll be penned up like animals and have nothing to do. No wonder they break out," the soldier lamented. "To think that I'm building a career on the bodies of these people."

Ricardo changed the conversation. "Tell us about the promotion,"

Fredericks smiled self-consciously. "It was touch and go at first. When they found out that Beeshore had lost all those men and not killed any of the enemy in return, the officers called a board of inquiry. Luckily, I was exonerated, because I wasn't with the group that got it. Then, for some reason, they made out that it was my idea about the trap you planned."

"What do you mean?" Ricardo asked.

Fredericks took off his hat and ran his hand through his blond hair. "I tried to tell them that it was your plan and that I was just following your advice. Two of the senior officers took me aside and ordered me to remain silent about your part in forming the battle plan. They said the country needed heroes right now, and especially this U.S. Army command in the Arizona Territory. As you know, we haven't always been too successful in our campaigns."

The Montoya brothers smiled.

"It's all right," said Ricardo. "Remember, the plan couldn't have worked as well as it did if your cavalry had not participated."

Fredericks beamed, and freckles stood out on his fair face. "My picture was even run on the front pages of some of the eastern newspapers. They blew the story all out of proportion, but my parents loved it. I was promoted ahead of schedule, and the newspapermen and their cameras are waiting for us at the fort."

Rafael turned his head and looked at the squaws and children in their dirty, bedraggled state. "They're not much to take a picture of."

The cavalry captain looked a little disheartened. "Aren't there any braves left alive?"

"In Mexico," said Ricardo. "Five or six got away with half a dozen women and children. Out of the whole group of two hundred, there are only about twenty-five or so left alive.

Fredericks glanced at Ricardo and then back at the Apache prisoners. "I can see the headlines now: SOLDIERS SLAY 175 SAVAGE MARAUDERS."

An hour later the cavalry troop mounted and left with their captives. Rafael and the vaqueros prepared to depart.

"Are you sure you won't come with us?" Rafael asked his brother.

"I'm sure."

Rafael grinned. "The girls are beautiful in Hermosillo this time of year. They bloom like the flowers."

"At least I won't have trouble finding you," Ricardo said, and smiled.

The brothers embraced, and Rafael mounted his horse and led the Mexican cowboys back to their own country.

Ricardo mounted Oro and headed northeast toward Patagonia and the Barringer Ranch.

***

Victoria Barringer sat across the table from her son. She observed his rough table manners and the haste with which he downed his food.

"I do wish you would relax a little at the dinner table, John. You're acting as if you can't wait to get away," she said with a slight smile.

John jerked his bushy black head up from his plate and glowered at his mother. His large eyes were always filled with a sullen anger that accented the perpetual scowl on his harsh face. He eyed his mother suspiciously.

"You've been spending a lot of time in Tucson lately," Victoria said in her perfectly articulated speech.

"So what?" John growled.

"You've been losing heavily at the gambling tables, haven't you?"

"Look! I do what I want, Mother."

Victoria carefully inspected her son. She placed her elbows on the table and touched her fingertips together under her chin.

"John," she said in a calculating voice. "I've ordered your credit cut off at all the gambling houses."

"You did what?"

Victoria's eyes narrowed. "You lost ten thousand dollars last month, John. Your debts have been paid, but I've put a stop to any more losses."

He choked down a mouthful of food and his face grew red. "You've gone too far!" he shouted.

"Calm yourself. You're a poor gambler, and the ranch cannot afford to support incompetence," she said.

"Don't talk to me that way," he snarled.

Victoria had a way of maneuvering, taunting, and scheming as her systematic mind pursued a goal. She had a sly smile on her face now.

"I do give you credit, John. You have worked hard and managed this ranch well. We have expanded our boundaries and are continuing to grow," Victoria said in a magnanimous voice.

The bearlike man scanned his mother's face to determine if she was being devious. As usual, he could not read her expression.

"However," she said in an energetic voice, "you do have your weak points."

"What do you want?"

"If you're looking for a trade, forget it," she said, and sat back in her chair. "There are a few changes I want made."

"What are you talking about?" he asked suspiciously.

"I'm talking about your attitude, primarily. I want you to be civil to the help. We've lost too many good servants because you treat them so badly."

"What do I care about those beggars?"

Victoria gazed at her son. "You have so little regard for people, John. I don't understand how you can be so devoid of a conscience."

John Barringer glared at his mother with open dislike. "You never cared about me. No one did. It was always Bob. He was the one you and Father were so proud of. He couldn't do any wrong in your eyes. And, what about me? I was always there, and I couldn't do anything right. Nothing seemed to please you," he said bitterly.

"Was it always a contest?" she asked quietly.

"Yes!"

"I thought we treated you equally," said Victoria.

"Never! You didn't even look at us the same way. When you looked at Bob and talked to him, you smiled. You never smiled at me," he growled.

"Well, you were always in trouble of one kind or another."

John sat in the chair, and his large, tense body appeared to lose its hostile pose for a moment. "It was no fun always being the other son. The one that was never quite good enough."

"I'm sorry, John. I really am," Victoria said sincerely.

"It's done," he said with a note of finality.

"And what of William?" she asked.

"What about him?" he asked.

She noted the look of distaste that flashed over his face. "He is your son. Yet you treat him like a lackey?"

"He looks like her," John replied.

"You mean your ex-wife?"

"Yes. And he doesn't like me at all. He would have gone with his mother if I'd let him. Now I wish I had," he said angrily.

"Perhaps if you treated him better, his opinion of you would improve."

John shook his head, and his eyes blazed. "I don't care what he thinks of me. I don't care that he's alive."

Victoria watched her son closely. "There's another matter we must discuss today."

John threw his napkin on the table and prepared to rise. "I'm through talking."

"James is on his way back to the ranch," she announced.

Barringer stared at his mother and his body went rigid. "I don't want him here. If he comes back here, I'll kill him," he growled. "I don't recognize him as being any blood kin of mine, and I won't have him around."

Victoria entwined her fingers and looked her son straight in the eye. "He is coming back, and you are to leave him alone."

John snorted and gave her a menacing look. "He's making his last ride then."

"I was afraid of that, so I had my will changed when I was in Patagonia," she said, and smiled.

"You did what?" he snarled.

"I changed my will. If James is harmed, you are automatically written out."

"You're joking," he said incredulously.

"I've never been more serious," she said in a loud voice. "You can check with our attorney, Harry Palmer, to verify that fact."

A violent rage was building up in John Barringer. "This isn't funny," he bellowed.

Victoria was regal and unflappable in the presence of even the most formidable adversary. "It would be too much to expect harmony to prevail. But I will not tolerate members of the family attempting to kill one another. From this moment forth, there will be no more chicanery, no more plotting, and no more violence."

John was speechless and his mouth hung open.

Victoria's determination to stop bloodshed was wielded with the same forceful action she had used to construct and mold the Barringer empire. She never swayed from exercising total power over all who came in contact with her.

"Close your mouth, John. It's time to resign yourself to the fact that there will be another Barringer helping to shape the destiny of this ranch," she said.

"You haven't heard the last of this," he threatened.

"I've heard all I want to hear. The subject is closed," she emphasized.

John grunted and charged out of the room.

Victoria rang the small dinner bell beside her plate. A maid appeared and discreetly removed the fine china. She sipped her coffee, lost in her own thoughts. A few minutes later, she rose from the table and went out on the veranda. Early evening, with its fresh breezes, was her favorite time of the day. She sat there for some time, rocking gently in her chair.

Just as the sun began to drop over the horizon, she saw a lone figure sitting on a palomino at the crest of one of the small hills that surrounded the ranch house.

"Just like his grandfather," Victoria said to herself. She remembered how her husband had often stopped on his way into the ranch so that he might view his holdings in the fading twilight. He had been so proud of what he had accomplished.

***

The figure rode slowly across the prairie, around the outlying buildings, and up to the house. James had changed into Arizona cowboy clothes and so had his identity changed. He stopped in front of his grandmother. The two studied one another in silence.

He regarded her with a mixed look of admiration and wariness. Never had he met a woman like her, and he never expected to again.

"Hello, Grandmother."

She smiled and stopped rocking. *If I can only get him to stay long enough, I'll turn him into a true Barringer,* she thought.

"I'm glad you're back, James."

They sat and talked about the family, his father and mother, and the ranch, and how it was continuing to grow in size. Twilight turned to darkness, and the servants lit candles and lanterns. James was all but mesmerized by her melodic, flowing yarns. She talked effortlessly, but at the same time her eyes were probing, analyzing, and digesting.

She reached over and patted his arm. "I don't think I've allowed you to say much at all this evening, James," she said, and smiled.

James sat back and sipped a cool drink. "I'm tired, Grandmother. It's nice just to sit here and relax."

"Tell me about what you've been doing and where you've been," she said.

James told her about his encounters with Sky Walker's band, the cavalry tragedy, General Vorshoff's participation, and finally about bringing the survivors back to the United States.

"You mentioned that Don Diego Salazar was killed. Could you go back to the hacienda?"

"No," said James. "Don Diego's son, Francisco, now runs the ranch. Tradition and pride would not let him accept me back at the hacienda. His father and I became bitter enemies, and therefore I became his enemy. The insults that I perpetrated upon his father, imagined or otherwise, leave no room for forgiveness under the rules that govern our culture."

"What about your brother, Rafael?" she asked.

"That's different. Don Diego trusted him until they had a falling out at the end. Francisco likes Rafael and often went to him for advice. I know Rafael would like to go back. It's his home."

Streaks of light and shadow from the flickering veranda lanterns crossed her face, giving exaggerated depth to her features.

"Are you saying it's no longer your home?" she said, studying his reaction closely.

James was silent for a moment.

"I can't go back," he said, his voice sad but decisive.

Victoria's smile was one of triumph. "Well, that's that," she said in a crisp voice. "I always say, one must look to the future. I made an addition to my will that disinherits John should violence surface. That should make things easier around here."

James gave her a skeptical look. "I still intend to find out who killed my real mother and father."

"Obviously, I think you're wasting your time. Everything was too long ago. But do what you think is best. Just don't look for trouble," she cautioned.

William Barringer stumbled as he walked out onto the veranda. The young man looked fearful as he glanced at James.

"Could I...could I bother you for a moment, Grandmother?" he asked shyly.

"Of course, William," she said in a patronizing voice.

"Is it all right if I ride into Patagonia with the supply wagon tomorrow? There are some things I wanted to buy," he said.

The tall, awkward youth had large, sensitive brown eyes. His expression alternated between wistful and apologetic as he shuffled his feet. He looked quickly at James and then glanced at his grandmother. James was impassive as he scanned the young man, but seemed to recognize that he was very insecure. Victoria was watching James as he viewed his cousin.

"Yes, you may," she said in a good-natured voice. "Sit down with us, William. I want you to get to know James."

"I...I...I should be going," he said nervously as he looked down, avoiding James's eyes.

His grandmother sensed what the young man was thinking. "It's all right. Your father and I have come to an understanding about James." Victoria told a wide-eyed William about the addition to her will. "It's only fair that you know," she stated.

William had been used as a pawn by his father and grandmother during their numerous confrontations over the years. His father beat him brutally at times, verbally abused him on a daily basis, and showed him no love. His grandmother exercised her substantial intellect to maneuver him like a puppet in her schemes. Now Victoria realized that he needed guidance and someone to admire. His manhood was upon him, and a proper role model was vital.

"The roundup is only a few days away," said Victoria. "John left in a huff, and I don't think he'll be back in time to direct it. James, would you organize the venture?"

James looked surprised. "Yes," he said.

"William needs some training. Would you do me another favor and let him accompany you?" she said, and gave James a sly look.

The youth sat up straight. "Oh! I'm not experienced enough. I really wouldn't be much good."

James smiled. "I could use some help. There are a lot of people and places I don't know about. You could provide me with the information."

William was unaccustomed to being accepted as an adult or being asked to contribute. But he seemed to like it.

"Yes...sure," he said as he studied James.

Victoria outlined the basic plan for rounding up the cattle on various ranges. William knew all the surrounding country and spoke knowledgeably about the terrain and topography. He had spent many hours out riding by himself in order to escape his father, and had found a second home on the prairie.

Victoria watched the two men talk and was glad to see that they were establishing a rapport. She excused herself and moved quietly into the hallway. She stopped halfway up the stairs to the second floor and listened to the faint voices of the men. William had found a listener and was eagerly pouring out his considerable energies and long-repressed ideas. Victoria retired to her bedroom and went to bed, falling into a deep, peaceful sleep.

LEE BISHOP

CHAPTER 17

The closeness of the two men grew as the days passed and the range crews began the roundup and branding of calves. William stuck to James like glue, and James gave him instruction in roping, branding, and the use of firearms. The youth was a fast learner and a hard worker. A compliment from James would always bring a quick smile to William's face. As his confidence in his own abilities grew, he became more outgoing and friendly.

After the first few days, James had no trouble with the cowhands. His experience in running crews of cowboys was evident, his abilities were superior, and he carried himself and conducted his actions with total confidence. The men welcomed James as a relief from the explosive, ill-tempered John Barringer.

William took his share of good-natured kidding from the cowboys, but he handled it well, and by the end of the second week he was fairly well accepted. The only reluctant one was Tad Carson, a burly cowboy who continually sniped at the young man with remarks intended to embarrass him.

Carson had been one of John Barringer's followers and had received favored treatment over the years. He looked upon James as only temporarily in command, but he did not have the courage to oppose him. Instead, he took it out on William.

After listening to Carson's particularly lengthy taunting of William over his inexperience in roping, James dumped the contents from his coffee cup and set it down hard on the step of the chuck wagon.

"Are you about finished, William?" he asked.

"Yes," said the young man.

"Then, go over and spell Green. Send him in for lunch," said James.

William complied immediately, obviously glad to get away from Carson's ridicule.

James watched him ride off. He turned and looked at Carson, who was slowly chewing his food, a nasty smile on his face.

"Carson, come over here," said James.

The cowhand took his time setting down his plate, getting to his feet, and walking slowly over to James. More than a dozen cowboys were sitting and reclining around the campfire. They all stopped eating to watch.

Carson had a self-satisfied look on his face as he gazed at the new head man. James pulled out a wad of money, counted out several bills, and threw them on the ground.

"You're through, Carson," he announced in a loud voice.

Carson's expression changed from bewilderment to anger. "You can't fire me. I work for John Barringer."

James's right hand lashed out as he slapped Carson across the face. The force of the blow almost knocked the cowhand to his knees. He shuffled his feet to keep from falling.

"Pick up that money," James ordered. "Get on your horse, and get out of here."

Carson shook his head several times to clear the fuzziness. He looked into James's eyes, which glittered with fury, and fear crept over his face. The cowboy slowly bent down and collected the money, backed away, and walked unsteadily to his horse.

Once he was mounted, Carson flashed a look of hatred at James.

"You ain't seen the last of me. I'm joinin' John Barringer and his own private roundup. When he comes back, you'd better be gone," he yelled.

Carson spurred his horse and rode away. James looked at the cowhands, wondering what Carson was referring to. Cap Ousterhout, an older man whom James had come to rely on, would not meet his eyes.

Later in the day, James had an opportunity to be alone with Ousterhout. He rode up to the cowboy, who was riding the right-point position as the herd moved back toward the ranch headquarters. Ousterhout was a weather-beaten, sinewy cowhand, his big nose and ears perpetually red from the sun. Small, brown eyes peered out from a mass of wrinkles.

"Things are moving pretty good," James commented as he took off his hat and mopped his brow with his sleeve.

"Yeah," said Ousterhout.

Barringer inspected Ousterhout closely. The old man had a cigarette dangling from the corner of his mouth and gave his full attention to the cattle drive.

"Do you know what Carson was talking about?"

Ousterhout's lips tightened on the cigarette, causing the glowing tip to rise. "Wondered when you'd get around to askin'."

"The sooner I find out what's going on, the sooner I can stop it," said Barringer.

Ousterhout glanced at Barringer for a moment, then looked at the cattle. "You can't do nothing now. It's too late," the old man said.

"Mind explaining?"

Ousterhout turned in the saddle and looked intently at James. "I been givin' it some thought, as to where does a man's loyalty lie. I come to the conclusion that it ain't with John Barringer, so I'm goin' to tell ya. But just forget where you heard it."

"I've already forgotten," said James.

"He's done it before, I hear. When he needs money, he gets a crew of men from Tombstone and they round up some cattle and sell them to the miners. I heard rumors, and I don't know if it's true, that he's in the midst of takin' a big chunk of cattle off the northeast range and drivin' em to the mines," said Ousterhout.

"It's bound to be discovered," James noted.

The cowhand shrugged his shoulders. "What kin she do to him? She can't hang him."

Later that day the herd reached the central roundup point on the range, two miles north of the ranch house. James and William continued on into the headquarters.

Victoria was on the veranda watching the men as they rode in. William went inside, leaving James and Victoria alone together.

"And how is your protégé doing?" she asked in a charming voice.

"Very well," said Barringer. "He's a fast learner, and I think he likes the work."

He took off his hat and sat down in one of the big chairs. "There's something I want to talk to you about. I've heard that some of the men believe John is taking cattle from the northern ranges and selling them to the miners around Tombstone and Bisbee."

Her penetrating blue eyes did not show surprise. "Really," she said.

"You don't seem surprised."

"I've known about it for some time," she said.

"What do you want done?"

"Nothing. If there's one thing we have plenty of, it's cattle," she said.

"If you let it continue, others will get the idea that this ranch does not protect its own. If he's allowed to continue to steal, it will invite other rustlers," said James.

"And what would you suggest?" she asked.

"Confront him with it."

"And then what?" she asked. Her eyes narrowed.

James riveted his gaze on her. "You don't want to stop it, do you?"

"It doesn't worry me if he takes a few cattle here and there," she replied.

"I'd stop him."

In her ever-so-subtle manner, Victoria said quietly, "Then do it."

James suddenly realized that she had trapped him. If he should force John out, it would obligate him to step in and run the ranch on a full-time basis, because William was certainly not ready.

Barringer chuckled, and Victoria smiled. "Someone has to run this ranch," she said.

James said nothing and looked out across the grasslands.

Victoria changed the subject. "How has your quest been coming?"

Barringer looked at her. "I've questioned every old cowhand and person who was alive back then. None of them could come up with the name of anyone who was thought to have been close friends with Scarface."

"Then you've about given up trying to find your father's second killer," she remarked.

James said nothing for a few moments. "It doesn't look too promising."

"Why not forget the past and look to the future?" she said brightly. "I understand there is a young lady who may fit into that future."

James smiled. "You never cease to amaze me with your knowledge of everything that goes on. Now you have sources in Mexico."

She gave him a sly look. "I didn't think you'd volunteer the information about Maria Bustamante."

James raised one eyebrow. "You even know her name."

"The information I pay for has to be accurate and complete. They say she is quite beautiful," Victoria remarked.

Barringer grinned and nodded.

William emerged from the house and stopped where Victoria and James were sitting. "I thought I'd ride over and see how the cattle count is coming. Is there anything else that needs to be done?" he asked James.

"No. I was just telling your grandmother how well you did on this roundup. You're turning into a regular cowhand," said James.

William beamed and walked toward the corral.

***

John Barringer and another rider suddenly rode around the side of the house and down to the corral. He glanced at the porch as he went by and noted that Victoria and James were there. William stopped saddling the fresh horse as his father dismounted and walked up to him. The young man looked worried and was suddenly nervous.

216

"They tell me you been out riding with him," John growled.

"Yes," William said quickly.

"Stay away from him. I don't want kin of mine going near that Mex," John growled.

William's mouth formed a firm line. "I like him, and I'll ride with him any time he'll have me."

"You swine!" the big man bellowed.

John lashed out with his quirt and struck the youth across the face. William doubled over and threw his arms up to protect his face. His father struck him twice more with the short whip. As he raised his arm a fourth time, a hand grabbed his quirt and jerked him over backward into the dust. John roared as he landed, then leaped to his feet.

"Why don't you pick on someone more your size?" James said in a challenging voice.

John glowered at James and grunted as he caught his breath. He had always been successful in street fights, and even now, as he neared fifty, John was still strong, tough, and gave no quarter. He sized up the tall man in front of him and judged that his own strength and bigger build would win out.

His head dipped slightly as he charged and grabbed James around the middle. John jerked his head up and smashed James under the chin. The two men reeled around like drunks. James held on, trying to clear his head. They crashed into the stable door and went through into the semi-darkness.

John grunted as he lifted James off his feet and used him as a battering ram. The door to one of the stalls shattered under the impact of James's weight. In close quarters, John's bullish weight and massive strength worked to his advantage as he drove blow after blow into James's face and chest.

James grabbed the big man around the knees, lifted him, and threw him over the wall into the adjoining stall. John bellowed just before he hit the ground. James waited for John to gain his feet and come out, his eyes narrow slits as he awaited his prey.

John charged out of the stall straight into a solid right cross that stopped him in his tracks. John tried to get his feet set under him, but James followed up with a left hook that snapped the big man's head back. James moved in close and pounded another hard right to the belly, followed by another left hook.

John groaned as he went over his back. He struggled to his knees and waited to catch his breath. His left eye was closed, and his face was a mass of blood and sweat.

Both men had lost their revolvers during the scuffle. John fumbled for his and realized it was gone. He summoned up his strength and charged James again. James easily stepped aside and clubbed John behind the neck. Barringer snarled as he went down.

John shook his head to clear the dizziness. His face was a hideous mass of red meat, with only one eye visible. He stumbled up and forward and grabbed a pitchfork from a haystack. "I'll kill you!" he shouted as he turned and confronted James.

James crouched down and started to back up.

"I should have killed you when I killed your stinking father. I'll correct that mistake now!" he yelled, and thrust the pitchfork toward James's stomach.

James had slowly been backing up prior to the charge and was in the stable doorway when John made his move. He jumped back and to one side, and John's thrust just missed him.

218

The men were outside again. James looked around for his revolver and saw it lying in the dirt. John came out and raised the pitchfork over his head for a final thrust as James dived for his weapon.

"Die!" Barringer roared, and drove the pitchfork at James.

James rolled over as one of the prongs sliced his side. At the same instant, he grabbed his revolver and fired into the big man's chest. John swayed above him for a moment and then collapsed. James held his bloody side with one hand and turned Barringer over with his foot.

The big man was dying. A deep rasping noise accompanied his labored breathing.

Victoria and William came running up to them.

"I hate all of ya!" John growled, and died.

***

The funeral was held privately, with only the immediate family members attending. After John was interred, James went to William's room and knocked softly.

"Come in."

James opened the door and walked in. "I didn't want that to happen. I especially didn't want anything to destroy our friendship."

William pondered the statement for a moment, then gazed at James. "I'm glad he's dead. I'd never admit it to anyone else, but I am. That man wasn't a father to me. I hated him, and I've never hated anyone else or anything in my life. It was miserable for me every day that I was around him. You did me a favor, James. It won't bother our friendship," William said quietly.

"Do you still want to go with me on the cattle drive up to the army forts?" James asked.

A slight smile came to William's lips. "You bet."

James left and went down to the living room to talk with Victoria.

***

"Come in and sit down," she said. Her voice was almost gay, and she did not look as if she had just lost a son, but rather like she had just come from a party. She looked dazzling in one of her long, silk dresses. Her jewelry sparkled in the lantern light. "Don't look so serious," she told James. "I realize you had no choice in the matter."

James sat down but said nothing.

Victoria's eyes searched his face. "He was beginning to become too much of a problem. He'd lost sight of what was important," she said matter-of-factly.

"What is important?" he asked, a hint of coldness in his tone.

She fixed him with her penetrating eyes. "This ranch, this empire is all-important. John had lost sight of that."

"Before John died, he told me he killed my father. Did you suspect as much?" James asked.

"What I did know was that you would come out the victor in any clash with John. He just wasn't of your caliber. Some men are leaders. Others would like to be but lack the ability to perform. I think John's insecurities were magnified towards the end. He looked at you as being a better man than he was. Failure will make a man do strange things," she reasoned. "You have my ability to rise to the occasion and vanquish your opponent through intellect, will, and tenacity. There are few people like the two of us."

Victoria sat back in her chair and riveted her eyes on the magnificent glass chandelier. She exhaled sharply, and returned her gaze to James.

220

"Just as you did, I suspected it once you told me about the circumstances. But it was ancient history, and the ranch had to go on," she said in a strong voice.

"Did John ever have pearl-handled revolvers in a black holster rig?" he asked.

"Yes. Years ago. But he lost them gambling. Why?"

"My Mexican father said the second man at the ambush site was wearing those guns."

"I see. Well, that confirms it then," said Victoria. "Will you and William be moving the cattle tomorrow?" Victoria said as she abruptly changed subjects.

Anger blackened James' eyes. "What's wrong with you?" he stated loudly. "Are you so insensitive that finding out that one of your sons killed the other doesn't even upset you?"

Victoria was unmoved by the blistering rebuke. Her regal expression did not change. "James, I didn't get where I am today by being a soft, emotional woman. You possess the same inner strength as I do. We are both prisoners in the same shell."

James got to his feet. "I'll never be like you," he vowed.

She smiled. "You are like me! You let nothing stand in your way."

His anger seemed to be waning, and he sighed, as if surrendering in their battle of wills. He stared at his grandmother, unable to continue being mad at her. "Yes. We'll be moving the cattle tomorrow," he said, and left the room.

I cried and I mourned when Bob and his family were killed, she thought. *I'm not going to mourn for them a second time. The murderers are dead; it's time to move on.*

Victoria sighed. "Every family has its ups and downs, and we have had more than our share," she said quietly to herself.

***

During the next month, the Barringer cowboys delivered more than ten thousand cattle to six army forts and two Indian reservations. Rafael joined James in Bisbee for two days and then returned to Mexico. He had been invited back by Francisco Salazar to head the ranch operations at El Rancho Grande, and had accepted.

The relationship between James and William had not been altered by the death of John Barringer...they were still good friends. The most important part of William's training was watching James handle the cowhands. His rapport with the men was excellent, James's orders were never challenged, and the men accepted him totally. But, he kept a degree of separation between himself and the cowboys in a reserved manner, not unfriendly but somewhat distant.

"They have to understand you are the boss, not one of the gang. Confidence comes from experience. It comes from hard work and doing things well. You'll become more confident of your abilities as time passes," James told William as they were returning to the ranch after the last herd had been delivered.

William glanced at James. "You're leaving, aren't you?"

James continued to look at the setting sun. "You can do the job here. You don't need me anymore."

The sensitive young man flashed a weak smile. "I'm not worried about that. I'll miss you. I don't have many friends. You're one of the few people I look up to."

James realized how difficult it must have been for William to say those words.

"I consider you to be a good friend, and I don't have a lot of friends either," said James. "I'm going to Mexico to ask Maria Bustamante to marry me. Hopefully we will come back here to live on the ranch. I'll be here to help you."

"Does Grandmother know yet?" asked William as the men dismounted and walked up the veranda stairs at Victoria's mansion.

"I'm going to tell her now," James stated. He stopped walking and looked intently at William. "You let her know you are going to be your own man, make your own decisions, and do what you think is right. Live your own life. Don't let Grandmother dictate to you."

"I intend to," William said and smiled. "I appreciate what you have done for me, James."

A maid came out of the front door and hurried over to the men. "Mrs. Barringer needs to talk with the two of you. She said it's urgent."

CHAPTER 18

Victoria Barringer was seated behind her desk. She wore a light blue silk dress and matching jewelry, and looked every inch the matriarch of the Barringer empire. Her eyes were fixed on the small man seated in front of her.

Arthur Dinwitty nervously jumped to his feet and had a worried look on his face when the two men entered the room. His large, dark eyes showed fear. He was short, bald in front, and was sweating profusely. He was dressed in an old blue suit that was shabby and should have been discarded long ago.

"Arthur, these men are my two grandsons, James and William."

Dinwitty looked as if he wanted to make a run for the door.

"Pull a couple of chairs over here. He has quite a story to tell," Victoria noted.

James grabbed two chairs and arranged them next to Dinwitty, who slid back into his seat.

"Arthur Dinwitty is the chief accountant for the mining operation. William works with him on a monthly basis when they review the accounting books," she explained to James.

William said hello to Dinwitty, but the little man did not acknowledge the greeting. His full attention was on James, and he appeared to be about to panic.

Victoria interjected, hoping to move the conversation along. "He says he has been falsifying the books, and our net profit over the last three years should be double the approximate three hundred and fifty thousand dollars that the books show."

William looked surprised. Anger flashed across James's face. Dinwitty looked terrified.

"You mean the Barringer Mining Company has been cheated out of hundreds of thousands of dollars?" James asked.

"The books looked accurate to me," William said in a bewildered voice.

"Apparently, they are. James, let me give you a little background on the type of hydraulic mining we are involved in near Bisbee. I bought up quite a few mining claims in the area when placers or deposits of gold were found in the sand and gravel in the region. I hired geologists, and they all hinted that there could be a large deposit or mother lode in the mountainsides."

She continued with an effortless stream of facts about how hydraulic mining used jets of water to break down gold-laden gravel banks and washed the material through gold-separating devices called sluices. As it turned out, there were large quantities of placer gold embedded in the mountainsides near Bisbee, she explained.

Dinwitty sat with his hands together in his lap, staring at the floor.

"To supply the needs for hydraulic mining, it takes a great deal of water. I had two mountain reservoirs constructed at high altitudes. Long ditch systems were built to bring the water down to the mining site, where very large water hoses blast apart the mountainsides," she noted.

James shook his head. "The investment must have been huge."

"We are just at the point of breaking even," William stated.

James glanced at Victoria and noticed that she was very calm. Nothing appeared to upset her composure, not even losing hundreds of thousands of dollars.

"Tell my grandsons how you did it, Arthur."

Dinwitty's hands were in his lap and his shoulders were hunched.

Victoria's eyes bore into the little man. "Now, Arthur!" she commanded.

He jerked in his seat. "The system for stealing is called high grading or pocketing the best nuggets. A team of four men raked and hoed the material and picked out the largest nuggets just before the material entered the sluice, where the smaller nuggets were dislodged from the gravel. Just the smaller nuggets were recorded as being mined. It's one of the richest claims I've ever seen," he said in a voice that began to crack.

"Why are you telling us this story?" James asked.

Dinwitty raised his head and tears were in his eyes. "They killed him."

"Killed who?" James asked.

"My friend, Jacob Barton. Yates told me that Jake departed, saying he was going to San Francisco. He wouldn't leave me. He loved me, and I loved him," said Dinwitty in a barely audible voice.

"Yates is Carl Yates, the Mining Superintendent, who I hired to run the entire mining operation," Victoria stated.

James suddenly felt sorry for the hunched over wreck sitting next to him.

"Why would they kill him?" James asked.

"He headed the high grading group, and he was keeping some of the largest nuggets for himself. I think Yates found out," Dinwitty explained.

"Does Yates know you are here?" James asked.

"No. Yesterday, I saddled my horse and left the mining operation. I decided to come here. It's the only way I can get back at him. His name is not really Yates. I think his real name is William Graves. I read letters that Yates had in his desk. They were addressed to William Graves in St. Louis."

Victoria sat back in her chair. "I did extensive background checks on

Carl Yates. Everything showed that Yates was a well thought of geologist and mining executive."

"He could be dead, too. I think Graves took Yates's identity," said Dinwitty.

William and James glanced at each other. The revelation had taken them by surprise. James was thinking through a course of action when Dinwitty grunted and looked as if he was going to faint. Victoria poured a glass of water from a carafe on her desk. The small man drank the glass of water and became somewhat calmer after a few moments.

"What are you going to do to me?" he asked in a worried voice.

"For now you are going to stay here at the ranch. You will be guarded twenty-four hours a day. If you are willing to testify against Yates, I will ask the court that you not be sent to prison," Victoria responded.

"I will gladly testify against him," Dinwitty blurted.

The Barringers questioned Dinwitty for another ten minutes. Then, he was escorted to a small room in one of the barracks and locked up for the night.

Victoria looked from one grandson to the other. "What ideas do the two of you have?"

"Yates has at least six bodyguards," William pointed out. "When I've gone to the mine, they are all around the headquarters building. He told me it's because they are dealing with large quantities of gold, which makes sense."

"Going to the mine with a lot of cowboys could result in many of our men being shot. We need to try to get him to come here," James suggested.

"We are having a Mexican fiesta here a week from Saturday. I'll send a letter to Yates tomorrow inviting him and his assistant superintendent Brian Teeter to the fiesta. They are always together when I meet with them. I would imagine Teeter is involved in the thefts as much as Yates," Victoria pointed out.

James was quiet, thinking through what Dinwitty had told them. William and Victoria watched him attentively, saying nothing.

"He appears to be believable. The two of you know him. Do you think he is telling the truth?" James asked.

"Yes, I do," said William. "He's too frightened to be lying."

"One of the strongest motives is revenge. Poor Arthur is missing his friend and believes him to be dead," Victoria pointed out. "I think he is telling the truth."

"What's the purpose for the fiesta? It isn't a Mexican holiday," James noted.

Victoria smiled. "No. It's the celebration of two weddings. Two Anglo cowboys are marrying two young Mexican women. Members of the Mexican families have been good workers here in the house and on the range. Both of the cowboys have been with us for some time and are well thought of. I like to sponsor these fiestas because they are very colorful, a lot of fun, and the families deserve to have a good time."

James nodded his head in agreement with the idea.

"What if they turn down the invitation?" William asked.

James thought for a moment. "They won't turn it down unless they suspect that Dinwitty came here. If that happens, we'll have to use another strategy."

***

The grounds around Victoria's mansion had been transformed into a colorful pageant. Adornments included banners, beautiful streamers, Mexican and American flags, and dozens of tables set up and covered with multi-colored table cloths. Flowers made with bright-colored tissue paper were everywhere. Mariachi music added to the festive atmosphere.

Enchilada, tamale, and taco buffets were set up with side dishes of refried beans, tortilla chips, and salsa, plus mounds of guacamole. Kegs of beer were scattered at stations around the grounds.

A portable dance floor had been put down and game tables had been set up for the children. Piñatas hung from poles. Rows of chairs had been set up under tent-like ceilings to protect the participants from the sun. The two couples were married in the Catholic Church that had been constructed on the ranch. Then, they all moved to the reception area and the festivities began.

Carl Yates and Brian Teeter had accepted Victoria's invitation.

Yates was six feet tall, had broad shoulders, salt and pepper hair, and a broad, handsome face with a ruddy complexion, large brown eyes, and a strong nose. Yates carried himself with confidence. His blue suit, shirt, and tie were immaculate, and his shiny, black shoes completed the mining superintendent's attire.

By comparison, Teeter seemed almost invisible. He was shorter than Yates, dressed in a simple brown suit that was common but did not stand out. His face was average, not one that people remembered. Teeter was the type of man a person could walk past and never remember seeing. Only one characteristic stood out…Teeter was a chain smoker, who lit one cigarette after another and stopped only when he ate.

Victoria greeted the men when they rode up to the ranch. Drinks were served on the veranda. Music and festivities encompassed the trio, and any misgivings the mining executives might have had were defused. William joined the trio and was warmly greeted by Yates. James walked up to the group, was introduced and shook hands with both men, and joined the gathering.

***

An hour later after they had eaten, Victoria suggested they return to her office to go over some paperwork. As they sat down around the large table, Yates thanked her for the invitation.

Victoria wasted no time and went directly to the heart of the matter.

"Carl, a man named Arthur Dinwitty paid us a visit. William works with him on a monthly basis. He's your head accountant and claims you have been high grading the ore and pocketing a large amount of gold. He said this has been going on for three years."

James noticed that the two men reacted differently. Yates shook his head, indicating that the allegations were not true. Teeter's eyes became mere slits as he stiffened in his chair.

"That's just not true, Victoria. We have had an excellent relationship and everything I have done has been honest and straight forward," Yates said in a convincing manner.

"What about Mr. Dinwitty?" she asked.

"He left the mining operation and apparently came here. Lately, he's been unhappy. I thought he might quit and leave the company," Yates stated.

"Dinwitty also told us that your name is not Yates. He said your real name is William Graves," Victoria asserted.

Yates responded by pulling some papers out of his suit coat.

"Here's some letters to me from our bank in St. Louis. These should prove who I am," said Yates.

He stood up and reached across the table to hand the papers to Victoria.

James was intently watching Teeter, believing him to be the more dangerous of the two men. He realized his mistake when Yates pulled a small revolver from his coat and pointed it at Victoria's head.

"Don't draw any weapons," Yates announced as he walked around the table and stood behind her. "I don't want to kill her."

Victoria had an angry look on her face, but she possessed the presence of mind not to get flustered. "James, don't do anything rash," she said quietly.

All eyes were on James Barringer. He had argued against a friendly meeting and had wanted to confront the men out in the open. But, Victoria prevailed with her argument that a business meeting should be held in the house.

Teeter stood up and drew a gun from his coat. James slowly rose from his chair. The color had gone out of William's face, and he did not move.

"You men need to get the hell out of here," James growled.

Yates's personality and temperament changed instantaneously. "Shut up! I make the decisions," he growled. "We're taking Victoria back to the mine. William, you collect two hundred thousand dollars from the Tucson and Tombstone banks. I know they will loan you any amount of money. Bring it to the mine in one week, and we will swap Victoria for the cash. She won't be harmed."

"No. You are not leaving here with my grandmother," James emphasized.

Victoria realized that gunplay was seconds away, and she did not want to lose her grandsons. "That's enough, James. I don't want you or William harmed. I'll go with them. William, you get the money from the banks, and we will make the trade," she told her grandsons.

"You can't trust these men—" James began, but was cut off by Victoria.

"Do as I say!" she commanded.

William got up from his chair. "Come on, James."

"Bring a buckboard around to the front of the house. We will leave immediately," Yates stated.

The Barringer men left the room.

***

Victoria rose from her chair and fixed Yates with a look of intense dislike. "You certainly had me fooled. I thought you were a man of honor, and you turned out to be a cowardly killer!"

Yates swung his hand hard, striking Victoria across the side of her head. "You rotten bitch. You think you own everyone, but not me, damn you!" he growled.

The strength of the blow had knocked Victoria to the floor. She shook her head, trying to focus as she slowly got up from the floor. After a few moments she fixed Yates with a blazing stare. "I'll hunt you down wherever you go!" she stated.

CHAPTER 19

The Barringer Mining Company buildings were on top of a small hill directly north of the mining operation. The large mining headquarters building was a long, flat-roofed rectangular building that faced the hydraulic mining across a small valley. Jets of water demolished the hillsides on a continuing basis. A variety of other buildings, including three bunkhouses holding twenty men each, were scattered around the hilltop. Stacks of lumber and steel and a large corral completed the mining site. The headquarters building had all windows covered with bars.

Victoria Barringer was confined to a bedroom used by mining guests. It contained a large bed, two chairs, and a small table. The large window to the outside produced a perfect view of continuing destruction of the hillsides through the use of hydraulic mining.

The matriarch attempted to escape during her second day of confinement. As a servant came into her room to collect the metal tray and dinner dishes, she purposely dropped a metal cup. The short, thin man bent to pick up the cup as Victoria swung the tray as hard as she could. The metal edge struck him in the forehead, knocking him to the floor, stunned, as blood ran down his forehead. She ran from the room and down the hallway towards the front door. Victoria entered the large great room, opened the front door, and ran into the nearby trees. But she could still hear the commotion when the servant began yelling, which brought Carl Yates and Brian Teeter running from a small room that housed the gold.

"She hit me with a tray," he moaned.

"You let an old lady knock you down?" Teeter said in an incredulous voice.

Then Victoria saw Teeter run outside, collect two guards, and head into the trees after her.

Victoria ran in a large circle around the buildings, heading for the corral. Her kidnappers had allowed her to take a riding outfit with her when they left her home, and she was wearing it now. The jacket and split skirt were made of medium brown calf skin that blended into the evening shadows, making her almost invisible at night. *If I can just get on a horse, I'll be out of here*, she thought. Victoria opened the corral gate just as Carl Yates grabbed her by the shoulder. He whirled her around and smashed her across the side of her head, knocking her unconscious. The last thing she heard as she faded was Yates's voice as he snarled, "That'll teach you to try and run from me, you rotten bitch."

***

James Barringer and Silk Mathews were both using binoculars to study the layout of the mining buildings. Barringer had brought Mathews with him because the former Confederate Army officer was an extraordinary marksman and one of the top hands on the Barringer Ranch. They were lying on top of a slightly higher hill, viewing every movement at the mining headquarters.

"Are you sure you want to do this?" Mathews asked.

"There's no way Yates will let her live. He'll kill her for sure. How would you like to have my grandmother chasing

236

you every day for the remainder of your life? That's the type of woman he kidnapped."

"She is a determined lady," Mathews observed.

"There are too many guards around the perimeter of that building for a daylight attack to be successful," James noted. "The two men on top of that flat roof are usually walking around or sitting down. At night, I'll bet they are asleep most of the time."

"Now would be the time to try to rescue her. It's three days before the trade, and they wouldn't be expecting us to try and free her," said Mathews.

"Did you see any ladders tall enough to reach the roof?"

"That building to the left has supplies and equipment. I would think there would be a ladder inside," Mathews stated. "The roof is about twelve feet high."

Barringer rolled onto his side and looked at the thin cowboy. "You are not obligated to go with me tonight. The odds that we will be successful are not the best."

"The chance for success will be a lot better if two of us participate. Besides, it's a challenge," Mathews said.

James laughed, and Mathews smiled.

The two men from the Barringer Ranch took turns sleeping until darkness set in. The shifts were four hours apiece for the guards. After nightfall Barringer and Mathews worked their way close to the mining camp, planning their attack for the early morning hours when the guards would be most vulnerable. The two o'clock shift involved six guards, one on each side of the structure and two men on top of the headquarters building. Barringer and Mathews located a ladder and waited another hour before they advanced towards the building. The night was overcast, and the moon was barely visible.

The guard at the rear was asleep. He sat with his back against the building, his chin on his chest. James swung his revolver and smashed him on top of his head, causing the man to grunt and fall on his side. Barringer and Mathews retraced their steps, picked up the ladder, and moved to the building. They had covered the ends of the ladder with rags to muffle any noise.

James quickly moved up the ladder and looked over the edge of the low wall around the top. One man was fully stretched out, asleep. The other was at the far end of the roof, looking skyward. Barringer moved quietly to the prone guard and hit him over the head. The second guard heard the noise and raised his rifle just as Mathews shot him through the chest.

Barringer and Mathews raised the trap door and quickly descended the stairs to the great room underneath. They ran down the main corridor, opening doors on both sides as they searched for Victoria. A man came out of one room with a revolver in his hand, and James shot him through the heart. One door was locked.

"I'm in here," Victoria called out.

"Stand away from the door!" James shouted.

Twice he kicked the area around the doorknob. The sash came apart the second time and the door swung open. James grabbed Victoria by the arm, and the three ran back to the great room.

"I knew you would come! I knew it!" she exclaimed. Her face was badly bruised but her vitality was intact.

Teeter, in pajamas and half-asleep, appeared at the opposite end of the office with a revolver in his hand. He raised his gun just as James shot him in the chest. Teeter was driven backwards against the wall and fired twice as he went down, his shots finding the ceiling. James and Silk both fired second shots that did not miss.

Barringer walked over to his dead body, picked up Teeter's revolver, and placed it on a large desk.

Seconds later, Carl Yates ran into the room thinking his bodyguards were there to defend him. However, the outside guards were not inclined to rush into a building with so much gunfire in progress. Barringer and Mathews pointed their revolvers at Yates, whose mouth dropped open. Yates recovered quickly and bent down, putting his gun on the floor, then raised his hands.

"Well Victoria. Apparently we will be seeing each other in court. It will be your word against mine. You've won this round, but I will win the next," he said in a smug voice.

Victoria Barringer moved smoothly, almost gliding over to the desk. She picked up the revolver and approached Yates. The mining superintendent suddenly realized what she was about to do.

"No! Be reasonable, Victoria!" he said loudly. "Good God, woman...."

Her eyes were mere slits as she raised the revolver and fired a bullet through his forehead. Yates's body was propelled backward against the wall and slumped to the floor.

James was momentarily dumbfounded by the chain of events, his eyes wide and his mouth hanging open. Mathews couldn't believe what had transpired either. Both men were speechless.

Victoria's demeanor was one of an angry yet satisfied woman as she approached her grandson. She reached out and patted him on the chest.

"No man kidnaps me and lives to talk about it!" the matriarch declared in a strong voice. Victoria had prevailed once again.

ABOUT THE AUTHOR

Following college at The University of Missouri and a stint in the U. A. Army, Lee began a 15-year newspaper career at The Phoenix Gazette in Phoenix, Arizona. He wrote more than two thousand news articles and feature stories for The Gazette.

His main work emphasis was government and politics, and most of his career was spent writing about the Arizona State Capitol, the Arizona House of Representatives and the State Senate. Lee also covered the Phoenix City Council and Maricopa County governmental issues. He wrote numerous stories about prominent Arizona politicians including U. S. Senator Barry Goldwater, Speaker of the U. S. House of Representatives John Rhodes, and U. S. Senator Paul Fannin.

Lee had three novels published during and after his newspaper career, including Gunblaze by Leisure Books; the first book in the Border Legend series by Walker and Company, and Davy Crockett for Dell's American Explorers series.

He left the newspaper business to pursue a career in real estate and still owns a real estate company, Southwestern Homes Realty, in Scottsdale, Arizona.

Lee and his wife, Sue, have two sons and two daughters, who all live in the Phoenix and Tucson areas with their families. They have eight grand-children.

He is an avid outdoorsman who walks his boxers two to three miles each morning. Lee's favorite passion is hiking the Grand Canyon at least once a year. He also plays golf regularly.

Lee has returned to writing novels on a full-time basis and concentrates on southwestern historical fiction with action and adventure being the dominant focus.

He and his wife continue to reside in Scottsdale, Arizona.

www.ingramcontent.com/pod-product-compliance
Lightning Source LLC
Chambersburg PA
CBHW050029180626
46810CB00002B/644